"If anyone can show any just cause why Ava and Ryan may not lawfully be joined together, let them now speak..."

Jane leapt to her feet. "Stop! *I* know of an impediment to this marriage."

Stunned silence. The wedding party turned as one.

Jane ventured boldly down the aisle, her gaze fixed on the minister. "You can't marry this couple. You're going to ask them to promise to love and honor and forsake all others—but one of them is already committed to someone else!"

SUSAN NAPIER was born on St. Valentine's Day, so it's not surprising she has developed an enduring love of romantic stories. She started her writing career as a journalist in Auckland, New Zealand, trying her hand at romance fiction only after she had married her handsome boss! Numerous books later she still lives with her most enduring hero, two future heroes—her sons!—two cats and a computer. When she's not writing she likes to read and cook, often simultaneously!

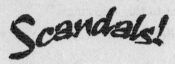

Have you heard the latest?

Get ready for the next outrageous Scandal

THE RANCHER'S MISTRESS
by
Kay Thorpe (#1924)

All will be revealed in December 1997

SUSAN NAPIER

Mistress of the Groom

𝓗arlequin 𝓑ooks

TORONTO • NEW YORK • LONDON
AMSTERDAM • PARIS • SYDNEY • HAMBURG
STOCKHOLM • ATHENS • TOKYO • MILAN
MADRID • WARSAW • BUDAPEST • AUCKLAND

ISBN 0-373-11918-6

MISTRESS OF THE GROOM

First North American Publication 1997.

CHAPTER ONE

THE tall, statuesque brunette wound her way sinuously through the glittering throng. Her formal black gown, cut low across her voluptuous breasts and deep to the base of her spine, flared out from her hips as she walked, the thin fabric shimmering as it slipped and slid against her long legs. Her hair was braided into a glossy black knot on the top of her head, adding to her already considerable height and emphasising the stark bareness of her white throat and shoulders.

The colour of her dress and her total lack of jewellery were in dramatic contrast to the rest of the women in the crowded hotel restaurant. The sought-after invitations from Spectrum Developments had placed an emphasis on glitz and glamour, and the female guests had taken the 'rainbow' theme to heart in order to flaunt their social and financial status at what was already being called Auckland's party of the year.

The woman in black didn't appear to be aware of her social solecism. Her head was held high, her pale, sharp features a mask of haughty calm as she ignored the whispers gathering in her wake, her icy blue gaze fixed on the small group of important men and vivacious women clustered around a towering figure at the far end of the room.

She was almost there when the tall man at the centre of all the sycophantic attention turned to pick up his half-full glass from the elegantly set dining-table beside him and caught sight of her.

His dark head lifted sharply, his nostrils flaring, his powerful muscles bunching within the sleek confines of his black-tie regalia as he shouldered through the mass of hangers-on to confront her approach. He looked like a stallion rearing at an unexpected intrusion into his territory—a massive black stallion, standing aggressively tall, radiating a restless antagonism, his spiky, short-cropped hair the same midnight colour as his superbly tailored jacket, his cobalt-blue eyes wild with untamed spirit, his blunt, masculine features hard and hostile.

Her stride briefly faltered and his expression changed to one of smouldering anticipation. His broad, flat cheekbones gave him a primitive look, the dark bloom on the smooth-shaven jaw adding to the impression of unbridled masculinity. She knew he had only just turned thirty-three but he looked older, with ruthless lines of experience etched around his eyes and mouth.

'Well, well, well...' he drawled in a darkly insolent voice as she came to a halt in front of him. 'If it isn't Miss Sherwood. I didn't realise you were on my invitation list. How tasteless of me to ask you to celebrate the man and the deal which sent your ailing little company to the wall.'

Jane Sherwood tilted her chin to an even more imperious angle, bitterly regretting that her three-inch heels still didn't give her nearly six-foot frame a height advantage over the sneering giant. They both knew damned well that she hadn't received one of the prized, hand-blown glass rainbows which had accompanied the engraved invitations.

'I wasn't invited, *Mr* Blair.' She echoed his parody of politeness with the full force of her loathing. Out of the corner of her eye she could see the white-jacketed hotel employee she had evaded at the door pointing her out to one of the guests, a wiry, hatchet-faced blond man whose grim alertness stamped 'security' all over him. Jane recognised him as the trouble-shooter who was never far from his boss's side, and as he began to forge towards them her nerves tightened another notch.

A hush had descended over the immediate vicinity as Ryan Blair's eyes crawled over the expensive designer dress.

'Ah, so *you're* the one being tasteless...although I must say you dress extremely well for someone on the brink of bankruptcy,' he said in the same insultingly condescending tone. 'I thought that the bailiffs would have been more rigorous in the performance of their duties—that dress alone would pay off a few of your numerous creditors...'

He raised his black eyebrows, his eyes reflecting the malice of his contemptuous smile. 'Considering the trouble you've taken to gatecrash, I'm surprised you haven't attempted to blend in with the colourful spirit of the occasion, but I suppose the black is supposed to be symbolic. I buried your company and now you're in mourning.

'Or is this martyred, monochrome look supposed to make me feel sorry for you? Have you come to beg for the crumbs from my table? I'm sorry, but as you can see—' he gestured mockingly towards the tables glittering with crystal and silverware '—we haven't dined yet. Why don't you call my secretary and arrange to see me at the office? If you're lucky I might be able to dredge up a few odd scraps to throw your way. I can't guarantee anything, of course, but then I'm sure you've discovered that beggars can't be choosers, can they, Miss Sherwood...?'

There were several titters in the background and a questioning buzz, but the protagonists were too intent on each other to be aware of the distraction.

'I didn't come here to ask for any favours,' denied Jane coldly, her stomach turning at the thought of being forced to beg before this sadistic swine. That was what he wanted, she realised sickly. Having stripped Jane of her family inheritance, her bright career and practically every material possession, he was now intent on exposing her nakedness to ridicule and contempt. As far as he was concerned this unexpected encounter was just another opportunity to grind her pride into the dust. Well, if she had to go down, she would go down fighting!

'No? Then perhaps you're here to *do* me one,' he taunted as their eyes clashed, two hostile shades of blue. 'It is my birthday, after all, and everyone else seems to be in a gifting mood. Have you come to give me something too, Miss Sherwood?'

'As a matter of fact, I have,' she said, stepping closer, her left hand momentarily concealed by the folds of her skirt.

Hatchet-face, who had glided silently up to his employer's side, stiffened and began to lunge forward, but he was halted by an out-flung arm.

'Really?' Ryan Blair dropped his arm as his would-be protector settled obediently back. 'I wonder what you could conceivably have to give me that I don't already possess?' The drawl was more pronounced than ever as he sipped from his glass of champagne, a picture of contemptuous relaxation, a man who was supremely confident of his enemy's impotence. And, no doubt because she was a woman, he was doubly certain of his superiority!

She realised she still possessed the element of surprise.

'This…!'

Even as she half turned away, dropping her left shoulder in a classic fighting gesture, he didn't seem to recognise his danger, and when her clenched fist came shooting up and out it was too late to duck.

The full weight of her feminine strength and fury was behind the punch which smashed squarely into his insolent jaw with a deeply gratifying crunch.

A jolt of excruciating pain exploded up Jane's arm and flashes of white light briefly dazzled her vision, but her smothered cry of agony was lost in the concerted gasp of the crowd and the female shrieks of dismay. Ryan Blair's head snapped back and the abrupt shift of his centre of gravity sent him crashing back against the round table behind him, his powerful bulk tipping it over and toppling him flat on the floor amidst a rain of crystal and cutlery.

The sight of him lying there cradling his bruised jaw, cursing like a navvy into the stunned silence, his façade of polished sophistication in ruins, was balm to Jane's lacerated spirit.

As the hotel events manager swooped down on the scene, gabbling horrified apologies, and the guests began to surge forward to help the man of honour to his feet, Jane turned her back on the chaos and walked out with the same calm, unhurried dignity with which she had arrived. She looked neither to left nor right, conscious of the path opening up before her as people drew back, afraid that their proximity to a social and business pariah might be interpreted as support. Ryan Blair had made it clear that whoever was not wholeheartedly with him was against him. And, as Jane had already discovered to her cost, he made a bitter enemy.

She reached the heavy glass door to the hotel foyer without hindrance, but as she reached for the brass bar a masculine hand was there before her, pushing it open. She turned her head in a bare acknowledgement and was startled to see that it was Ryan Blair's blond hatchet-man assisting her passage to freedom. She half expected him to try to detain her, or at least warn her that she was going to be sued for full damages, but instead he merely inclined his head as she passed through the door, a peculiar glint of sardonic admiration in his silver-grey eyes.

When she stepped out into the street, the summer night enfolded her like a warm and humid blanket. The footpath was still slick with the light rain which had fallen earlier in the evening and she had to walk slowly

and carefully in her spiky heels, acutely conscious that
the glass wall of the hotel restaurant fronted the street,
allowing everyone inside a clear view of her progress.

She was almost to the corner, where she would turn
blessedly out of sight into the side-street where she had
parked her car, when she heard a scuff of sound behind
her.

Before she could react she was whirled fiercely round,
her arms held in a steely grip.

'Oh, no you don't!'

She looked up into Ryan Blair's blazing blue eyes.

'You didn't think you were going to walk off scot-
free, did you? Nobody throws a punch at me and gets
away with it!'

His voice was thick with rage and her eyes fell to his
battered mouth, where a trickle of blood revealed a split
in his swollen lower lip. The reddened puffiness ran
down the left side of his jaw; by morning it would probably be black and blue. Jane had always shunned violence, in her whole twenty-six years she had never
seriously sought to injure anyone, but now she felt a hot
burst of pleasure at the sight of the damage she had
caused to Ryan Blair's handsome face.

'I don't see what you can do about it,' she told him,
riding a brave surge of adrenalin, struggling to wrench
herself out of his iron fists. 'Unless you want to make
yourself a laughing stock by having me arrested for as-
sault!'

'You don't think people are laughing at me *now*?' he
snarled, his fingers tightening on her bare arms.

'Whose fault is that?' she choked, giving up the un-
equal fight and standing straight and tall within his punishing grasp, her eyes icy with scorn. 'You may be rich
enough to buy loyalty but you still have to *earn* respect.
Your campaign to drive Sherwood Properties out of
business was vicious and underhanded and commercially
questionable. I bet a lot of those toadies in there that you

bribed or intimidated into your circle of influence secretly enjoyed seeing you get a punch in the face. They're just too scared to admit it!'

She had reminded him of their curious audience behind the glass wall of the restaurant, but instead of looking their way he glanced over his shoulder. 'So you did it because you think you have nothing left to lose?' he grated. 'Think again, sweetheart.'

And he jerked her against his chest, crushing her hands between them, lowering his head and forcing her shocked cry back down her throat with his plundering mouth. One large hand burrowed up into her immaculate coiffure, dislodging the pins, the other arm wrapped diagonally across her back, his fingers sinking into the swell of her buttocks as he arched her into a classic clinch. His foot thrust between her teetering heels, his knees squeezing her trapped thigh, and when she tried to push him away with her fists a burst of pain in her left hand made her gasp, opening herself even wider to the rough intrusion of his tongue. She felt the sting of his teeth against her tender lip and, tasting blood, didn't know whether it was his or her own.

He made no pretence of passion—it was an exercise in pure male dominance—but there was no pretence about the kiss, either. It was no chaste theatrical illusion, it was deep, hard and shatteringly real. Strange waves of heat and cold battered Jane's senses, and she thought she was fainting when a white light like the one that had dazzled her in the restaurant suddenly began pulsing and whirring around her head.

Just as suddenly Ryan Blair let her go and, staggering slightly, Jane saw a grinning photographer backing away, flashing off a few more shots as he went. She shuddered to think of the images he had captured on film.

'What did you do that for?' she panted furiously, putting a hand up to the heavy fall of hair which he had wrenched adrift. His gloating smirk told her that he had known the photographer was approaching when he had grabbed her.

His gaze fell to the lush, creamy-white breasts, heaving with outrage above her deep, square-cut neckline. 'Why, to show the good people of this city that that punch had nothing to do with my business practices and everything to do with our private relationship.'

'We don't *have* a private relationship,' she ground out, giving up and wrenching out the rest of the hairpins, tossing her head so that the raven-black waves rippled down her back. She knew she looked nothing like the cool, controlled, fearless woman who had confronted him in the restaurant a few minutes ago. Now she was flushed and crumpled and thoroughly kissed, demoted to the rank of a frivolous sexual object.

'Tell that to them.' He nodded towards the press of fascinated faces on the other side of the glass wall. 'By tomorrow morning it'll be all over town that you and I conducted a messy lover's quarrel in public. The gossip columns'll be speculating as to how long our secret affair has been going on, and whether we're as competitive in bed as out. They might start wondering whether our business rivalry was a smokescreen that only turned into the real thing when the relationship started going sour.

'Some people might even suggest that the *real* reason Sherwood Properties crashed was because its managing director fell in love and lost all sense of perspective, a classic case of a female letting her hormones rule her brain...'

Oh, yes, the creaking male chauvinists who inhabited the upper echelons of the business establishment would be only too delighted to bandy that theory around their executive men's rooms, Jane thought furiously. Because she was young and a woman she had had to work long and hard for her success. Her driving determination to show everyone that she was more than capable of filling her father's shoes had made her a formidable competitor in the field of commercial property dealing in the past five years...and put many older and more experienced masculine noses out of joint. The old boy network would enjoy the chance to dismiss her past achievements by turning her into a washroom joke.

'You bastard,' she hissed, stricken anew by the savage injustice of his actions. 'Why are you *doing* this to me?'

He gave a bitter, incredulous laugh. 'You know why. Because it's pay-back time...'

Jane wrapped her arms around her waist, shaking her head in bewilderment. 'Isn't what you've already done to me payment *enough*? Thanks to you, I've lost everything. How long are you going to keep on *hounding* me like this?'

He thrust his face close to hers, his voice as smooth as exposed steel as he unsheathed his malice and gutted her of any expectation of mercy.

'Oh, you haven't lost quite everything, my dear; that comes later... You wrecked my marriage—now I'm going to wreck *your* life just as thoroughly. So say goodbye to all your hopes and dreams, Jane Sherwood, because your future is going to be very different from the one you had planned!'

CHAPTER TWO

JANE slumped in the driver's seat of her two-door car, her forehead resting on the steering wheel. The keys were in the ignition but she wanted to get control of herself before she drove home. She knew changing gear was going to be wretchedly difficult.

The agony in her left hand had settled down to a dull throbbing that flared into hot needles of pain whenever she flexed her fingers. It was probably going to be as swollen and bruised tomorrow as Ryan Blair's jaw. But it was worth it, she thought bitterly.

She had wrecked his marriage?

He had never even *been* married!

Halting a wedding ceremony was not the same thing as splitting up a husband and wife. When Jane had stepped in to prevent Ryan Blair and Ava Brandon from taking their final vows she had truly believed that the dramatic, last-minute intervention was the only way to save the bride and groom from making a miserable mistake.

A dynamic, self-made man like Ryan Blair wouldn't have been happy with someone as passive and retiring as Ava, and her gentle, sensitive friend would have had her quiet individuality crushed by his dominating personality. If Ava had been madly in love with her future husband Jane would have wholeheartedly supported the match, despite her own serious doubts about the couple's compatibility, but she knew that, far from being in love, Ava was intimidated by the man her ambitious, old fashioned, overbearing parents had pushed her into agreeing to marry.

Ava had said that Ryan claimed to love her when he had swept into her life and proposed, but the announcement, shortly after their engagement, of a Brandon/Blair financial joint venture and his hectic work schedule, which allowed them little time together during their six month engagement, had deepened Ava's misgivings.

However, as usual, instead of confronting the problem, Ava had taken the path of least resistance until the last possible moment, only to have her belated attempts to assert herself ruthlessly dismissed as bridal jitters.

The first Jane had known of the depths of despair to which her friend had sunk was the day before the wedding, when Ava had invaded her office in tears. In between her friend's savage draughts of Mr Sherwood's eight-year-old Scotch, which still stocked the office drinks cabinet, Jane had dragged out the sorry details, realising with a shock that it had been months since she and Ava had sat down and talked together. No...since she had taken time to really *listen* to what her friend was saying.

Although she had ostensibly taken over Sherwood Properties when her father had been forced into premature retirement by a heart attack, Jane had only been a figurehead. Mark Sherwood had remained the real power behind the throne, as ruthless, demanding and critical as ever, constantly questioning her performance and countermanding her decisions, never letting her forget who was in ultimate charge. His sudden death when she had been still only twenty-two had made it critical that Jane prove as quickly as possible to competitors, clients and employees alike that she was as good—if not better—than her father.

So she had started putting in twelve-hour days at Sherwood Properties' downtown office, constantly pushing to improve the business, and had felt vindicated when the company's profits had begun to burgeon in response to her ambitious plans. Vindicated but not satisfied. Success had been like a drug. The more she achieved, the higher the goals she set herself.

In the process, Jane's social life had dwindled to virtually nil. It had given her a strange chill to realise that Ava was not only her best friend, she was virtually her only real friend—the rest qualifying merely as acquaintances or colleagues. The guilt over her neglect of their friendship had made Jane boldly assure her sobbing friend that *of course* she'd help her think of a way to escape the imminent marriage, a way that wouldn't result in an irrevocable family breach.

Secretly, Jane had thought Ava's self-confidence might improve if she were temporarily estranged from her manipulative parents, but she had known that her insecure friend would go through with a marriage she didn't want rather than risk permanently alienating herself from her mother. Having lost her own mother at six, Jane had no wish to be responsible for depriving anyone else of their maternal bond.

Jane cradled her injured hand in her lap, swamped by the memory of that awful wedding.

It had been almost exactly three years ago, on a beautiful, sunny spring afternoon. The graceful old inner-city church had been bursting at the seams with society guests when Jane had squeezed nervously onto the end of the back pew on the groom's side, resisting the usher's attempt to seat her further forward. She had had the feeling she might need the fast getaway, whether her hastily conceived plan worked or not.

Although, as giggling schoolgirls, she and Ava had vowed to be bridesmaids at each other's weddings, Jane hadn't been surprised when Kirstie Brandon had excluded Jane from the official wedding party by insisting that family take precedence. Ava had been upset but, as usual, quite incapable of standing up for herself. Mrs Brandon was an extremely possessive mother and had never liked the influence that strong-minded Jane had

exerted over her precious only child during their time at
school together. Not that she had been overtly rude; she
had merely made it clear, whenever Jane visited, that
she was a guest rather than a family friend.

Mrs Brandon set great store by appearances, and Jane
was too tall, too plain, too outspokenly intelligent to con-
form to her view of a proper lady. If her father hadn't
been a wealthy businessman Jane suspected that the
friendship would have been squelched altogether, rather
than merely tolerated, but Kirstie Brandon's mercenary
streak was almost as wide as her snobbish one. It had
always seemed a miracle to Jane that the Brandons had
produced such a kind, generous-hearted offspring.

So, two petite teenaged Brandon cousins had been se-
lected to serve as Ava's bridesmaids along with her fiancé's younger sister, and three excited little flower-girls
and two sulky page-boys had completed the entourage.
When Jane had seen the extravagantly flounced pale
peach-coloured bridesmaids' dresses coming down the
aisle she had had one more reason to be glad not to be
part of the fateful wedding party. With her height and
colouring she would have looked disastrously over-
decorated in all those pallid ruffles.

After the ceremony a lavish reception was to have
been held on a hotel rooftop, with a helicopter booked
to whisk the happy couple away to their honeymoon.
The Brandons had spared no expense for their only
child's wedding, another reason why Ava had felt
obligated to sacrifice herself to their wishes.

In the event, there was no marriage, no reception, no
honeymoon, and Jane considered herself fortunate not to
have been slapped with the bills by the furious parents
of the bride.

She had sweated through the opening part of the very
traditional ceremony, deaf to the poetry and grace of the
lyrical words, glad of the large picture hat and embroi-

dered net veil that she had chosen to wear with her tailored cream suit.

From under the deep brim she had watched Ava enter
the church door on her strutting father's arm. Just before
she had taken her first step down the aisle Ava had
glanced across at Jane, and her frightened, apologetic
eyes and valiant, wobbly smile had said it all: she was
trusting Jane to do what she herself had been unable to
do.

They had been friends since kindergarten, blood-
sisters since High School, and Jane had always been the
natural leader of their various exploits, the one who
boldly carried out Ava's wishful thinking. Whenever
they had landed in some scrape it had been Jane who
had cheerfully shouldered the blame, shielding Ava from
the full fury of adult outrage.

The years had passed but their respective roles had
remained essentially the same.

Jane's mouth had dried when the minister had finally
uttered the words that she had been waiting for, the pro-
nouncement that was usually mere ritual.

'Therefore, if anyone can show any just cause why
they may not lawfully be joined together, let them now
speak or else hereafter forever hold their peace...'

He paused. The few seconds of silence seemed to
stretch into eternity. Jane watched Ava's fragile, lace-
clad shoulders stiffen and settle as if accepting a blow.
In the periphery of her vision she saw a stir in the opposite pew and was released from her frozen inaction.

She leapt to her feet and stepped out into the aisle just
as the minister drew his breath to continue.

'Stop! *I* know of an impediment to this marriage.
There's a good reason why it shouldn't go ahead!'

Stunned silence.

The wedding party turned as one.

Kirstie Brandon moaned and swayed in the front pew.
Jane ventured boldly down the aisle, her gaze fixed on

the slack-jawed minister, conscious of Ava's trembling relief but afraid to look her way in case she caught the eye of the rigidly stupefied man at her side. The minister was quite young, the hint of panic in his shocked expression indicating that the interruption was unprecedented in his limited experience and he wasn't quite certain how he was going to handle it. Jane knew... *The solemnisation must be deferred until such time as the truth be tried...*

She had lifted her chin, her cold, pale face a blur behind the opaque veil. 'You can't marry this couple— their vows would be a lie before God!' Her voice rang with the sincerity of her conviction. 'You're going to ask them to promise to love and honour and forsake all others, but one of them is already committed to someone else!'

Sensation!

The steering wheel dug into Jane's forehead as she rolled her head in negation of the real-life nightmare that had haunted her for three years. She had vaguely realised that she was going to make some powerful enemies that day, but she hadn't realised how truly implacable and remorseless Ryan Blair would be in his lust for revenge. Fortunately, although she was still *persona non grata* as far as the Brandons were concerned, so was Ryan Blair. The humiliation of the failed wedding had been something the Brandons had attempted to expunge from existence, and in doing so they had held themselves aloof from the ensuing hostilities.

For more than a year, long enough to allow Jane's fears of reprisal to fade, Ryan Blair had dropped out of sight, fighting desperately behind the scenes to regain the financial footing that he had lost after the simultaneous collapse of his wedding and the Brandon joint venture project, which had apparently been going to bring a vital infusion of funds into his company. He had moved to Sydney to restructure and rebuild his fortune, keeping such a low profile that when he burst back on the Auckland scene, wielding serious economic clout and considerable political influence, it had come as a nasty surprise.

Ryan Blair had come storming back with a vengeance. Time, far from tempering his attitude to Jane's untimely interference in his personal life, seemed to have forged it into an unyielding hatred. From the moment he had resettled in Auckland he had not allowed Jane a day's respite. He had stolen her clients, head-hunted her staff, undercut her percentages, bought up her mortgages, blocked her financing, competed for every tender—so successfully that she knew he must have inside information from her office—and made attending business functions a misery by pointedly snubbing her and her companions completely.

Disaster had seemed to dog her every business decision. Unsourceable rumours had begun circulating about her private life, her mental stability, the viability of her company. Within two years her formerly superbly controlled life had been turned into total chaos.

Jane heard a tap-tapping and raised her head to see a tentatively smiling man knocking on her window, gesturing for her to wind it down. She did so, thinking that he was a kindly passer-by intending to ask if she was ill.

'Miss Jane Sherwood?'

She frowned, the thick black eyebrows that gave her a perpetually serious look rumpling in puzzlement. 'Yes.'

He consulted the piece of paper he was holding. 'Jane Sherwood of Flat 5, 8 Parkhouse Lane? Formerly proprietor of Sherwood Properties?'

She experienced the sinking feeling that was becoming all too familiar these days. 'Yes, but—'

She was cut off as he thrust the paper through the

half-open window at her and at the same time deftly whipped her keys out of the ignition.

'John Forster of Stanton Security. This vehicle is under a repossession order. I'm afraid I'm going to have to ask you to vacate the car, Ma'am, so that it can be returned to its rightful owner.'

While she was squinting at the small-print, which told her that all vehicles registered to or leased by Sherwood Properties were now the legal property of the mortgagee, he opened the door and invited her to step out onto the pavement.

'But how do I get home? I live on the other side of town and I haven't got enough money with me for a taxi or a bus—' Jane began to protest.

'What's going on here?'

To her horror she saw Ryan Blair step into view behind the stocky repossession agent. That appalling kiss hadn't been enough; he obviously wanted everyone to think that they had gone off somewhere together.

'Nothing—'

'I'm repossessing the car. The lady claims she hasn't got any way of getting home.'

Jane blushed vividly as her denial mingled with the horrible man's blunt announcement. She raised her chin and glared.

'I'll drive you home.'

Her eyes widened before her thick black lashes fell defensively. 'Go to hell!' she snarled.

'Look, lady, you got a lift home—take it!' the stocky man advised. ''Cos you're sure not going anywhere in this car. See my mate over there? He's going to hitch it up to his tow-truck if you won't let me drive it away.'

As Jane turned her head to look at the shadowy figure leaning against the cab of his tow-truck on the other side of the road she heard a rustle, and suddenly Ryan Blair was plucking her out of the car and setting her down on the pavement.

'Get your hands off me!' she hissed, struggling belatedly.

'You really don't know when to give up, do you?' he said grimly, stepping out of range of her flailing arms. 'What did you think you were going to do, sit there and argue all night? Let the man do his job.'

'Let him do your dirty work, you mean!' she snapped, remembering how, barely more than a month ago, she had been escorted off the premises of her own company by a security guard to ensure that she took nothing from the office, not even her personal effects. Sherwood's was not a limited liability company, so literally everything she owned was forfeit.

Ryan Blair folded his arms across his broad chest. 'It's standard practice for a mortgagee to request that all assets be sequestered when a company goes out of business.'

'What about my evening bag? I suppose you're going to demand that be sequestered as well?' Jane said sarcastically, pointing to the small black beaded drawstring bag which lay on the passenger seat.

He picked it up and handed it to her. 'Come on, there's my car.'

A black limousine was creeping across the entrance to the long cul-de-sac. The driver must have orders to follow his boss wherever he went, thought Jane contemptuously.

'I'm not going anywhere with you,' she said.

'Are you asking me to give you cab fare?'

'I'd rather beg in the streets!'

Her defiant statement was punctuated by the roar of her car engine as it was driven smartly away.

'It might come to that,' he pointed out softly. 'A woman dressed like you...expensive, displaying a lot of flesh, obviously alone....you're bound to attract plenty of attention from the kerb-crawlers. Only they'll expect you to *earn* your taxi fare.'

Her throbbing hand tightened on her bag. 'Why, you—'

'Temper, temper, Miss Sherwood,' he said, stepping back and lifting his hands in mock fright. 'You're not going to hit me again, are you? I always thought you were as cold as ice, but you have quite a volcano seething under that chilly exterior, don't you?' He dropped his hands and his voice acquired a bored impatience that suggested he didn't care one way or the other. 'Now, do you want a free ride home or not...?'

Pride warred with expediency and pride won.

'Not!'

Head high, she skirted the limousine and began to walk up the hill in the opposite direction to the hotel, away from the centre of the city. All she wanted to do was get away from Ryan Blair as quickly as possible, then she would decide what was best to do. She was well past the theatre centre, and even though the night wasn't very far advanced there were few people on this section of the street and no stores open, but she knew she had to come across a phone box soon.

Her sense of isolation rapidly intensified as she hurried on her way. Her heels sounded very loud against the concrete pavement and she shied at a shadowy couple in a shop doorway. Deciding that it might be more prudent to walk nearer the streetlights, she had barely got a few hundred metres when a car-load of young toughs cruised noisily past and then backed up, the scruffy youths leaning out of the window and crooning invitations and suggestions that burned her ears.

Her lack of reaction finally caused them to tire of their sport and the car roared away, spewing howls of raucous laughter, but almost immediately another one slowed to a crawl beside her. This time the suggestions from the lone driver were a great deal more sophisticated, but no less persistent and stomach-churningly graphic. At the end of her tether, Jane bent and rested her good hand on the open car window and delivered a blistering tirade to the sweaty, middle-aged man behind the wheel.

An obscene smile split his rubbery lips and he reached over and clamped his fat hand around her wrist. 'Yes, I know. I've been very bad and I must be punished. I knew when I saw you striding haughtily along that you were a woman capable of the most delicious cruelty. I look forward to your discipline—'

'Sorry, the lady's already booked up for the night!'

For the second time in half an hour Jane found herself the object of an unwelcome rescue. Ryan Blair's limousine was riding the bumper of the kerb-crawler as the man himself put his arm through the driver's window and hauled the culprit up by the shirt-collar to utter a few sibilant phrases in his ear. As soon as he was released the unfortunate man rammed his car into gear and took off, burning rubber in the process.

Ryan Blair, still standing on the road, hands on his broad hips, said through his teeth, 'Get into the limo, Jane.'

Jane opened her mouth.

'Get in the car, dammit!' he exploded, 'Or I'll wrap that silky black hair around your throat and drag you there!'

'Bully!' she slashed back, not quite certain that he wouldn't do it. She moved with defiant slowness towards the open back door of the limousine. Her feet in the borrowed too-tight black stilettos were almost as painful as her hand, her crushed toes raw with blisters that chafed with every step.

'Stubborn bitch!' he said, climbing in opposite her. 'At least now you'll live for me to bully you another day.'

'Oh, yes, you like to draw the agony out, don't you? You probably could have destroyed Sherwoods in weeks instead of stringing it out for nearly two years,' she accused wildly, anything to take her mind off the pain that was turning into a burning nausea in her stomach.

'I could,' he said coolly, lounging back on the luxurious white leather. 'But it wouldn't have given me half so much satisfaction.'

His frank admission took her breath away. She collapsed back against the seat, hardly noticing as the limousine pulled smoothly into the sparse flow of traffic.

She thought of all the times over the past couple of years when she had been certain that she was going to triumph over his bitter adversity, only to be hit by another financial blow that tumbled her down into the dumps again.

But there had never been a chance that she was going to win, she realised numbly. Those brief periods of euphoric hope had been as much a part of his strategy as the devastating body blows, designed to encourage her to fight, to blind her to the ultimate futility of her struggle. And the competitiveness drilled into her by her father had ensured that she had played right into Ryan Blair's hands. In a sense, she had created her own torment.

'But Sherwood's wasn't just *me*,' she said through white lips. 'There were other people involved, people who lost their *jobs* because of you—'

His swollen mouth curved cruelly. 'No, they lost their jobs because of *you*.'

'My God, you're callous,' she said, shaken by the depth of hatred revealed by the comment. She had known that he despised her but she hadn't realised how much. If she had, maybe she would have been better equipped to predict the pattern of his revenge.

He shrugged. 'I expect to be able to pick up what's left of Sherwood's for a song... I've no doubt I can make it a viable enterprise again in a very short time and re-employ most of the staff.'

'Those who aren't already in your employ, you mean,'

she said bitterly. 'If you hadn't been getting inside information you wouldn't have found it so easy to destroy my company.'

'Precisely. But all's fair in love and war, isn't it, Miss Sherwood? As it happens, your staff's loyalty was pathetically easy to suborn... Did you know you weren't a very popular employer? Too much of a chip off the old block, I understand. ''Arrogant and intolerant'', ''incapable of delegation'', ''rigid and unapproachable'' were some of the more flattering opinions of your management style.

'You're looking rather pale, my dear. Perhaps you need a whiskey to wash down the unpalatable truth.' He opened a compact drinks cabinet and began to pour amber fluid from a silver flask into a crystal glass.

'I don't want anything from you.'

'So you said. But there's no gallery here to play martyr to, no one to care whether you show a glimpse of human weakness.' He thrust the glass towards her.

'I said no.' She turned her head haughtily away. She hadn't had anything to eat since breakfast and, even if she could bring herself to take anything from his hands, the alcohol would probably hit her like a freight train. She didn't want to be any more helpless in front of him than she was already.

Had she really come across to her staff like an unfeeling robot? No, he was just saying those things to hurt her. They weren't true. She had wanted Sherwood's to be the best, and in striving to achieve her goals she had expected a lot from her employees but no more than she demanded of herself. Far from being a carbon-copy of her dogmatic father, she had wanted to stamp her own personality on the company, but real-estate was a dog-eat-dog business and the relentless pressure she had been under had necessitated her putting aside her new ideas in order to concentrate on the fight for sheer survival.

'Suit yourself. Ah, well...here's to the sweet taste of

victory,' he toasted her, and drank with robust pleasure, not flinching as the raw alcohol flowed over his split lip.

Everything about him was big and brash. There was an offensive vitality about him that contrasted with her own wilted state.

Jane remembered how uncomfortable Ava had been with his restless volatility, his constant need to be challenged, the natural aggressiveness which charged his character and made him a dangerous man to cross. Being engaged to him had been acceptable when they saw little of each other, but when he had started winding down his business activities closer to the wedding Ava had found herself unable to cope with the everyday reality of his forceful nature.

Jane had understood her fear, even though she didn't share it. She had disliked Ryan Blair for reasons of her own but she had never been afraid of him. Even now she was more furious than fearful, for she knew that her own strength of character would carry her through this crisis, as it had through previous tough times in her life.

He lowered his glass and stretched out his long legs so that they brushed insolently against hers. 'So...what are your plans now that Daddy's little heiress is broke and unemployed?'

'Do you think I'm going to tell *you*?' she said, swivelling her hips so that her legs were no longer touching his, resenting the implication that she had been a spoilt brat for whom life had been cushioned by privilege.

His blue eyes glinted in the passing slash of a streetlight. 'I'll find out anyway.'

She didn't answer, merely gave him the icy look of contempt with which she habitually hid her fears and insecurities.

'Of course, your options are rather limited, aren't they?' he mused silkily. 'The word is already out that anyone who offers a helping hand to Jane Sherwood could find themselves in the same mire. I think ''unemployable" rather than "unemployed" is a better description, don't you?'

She had already discovered the extent of his influence in her fruitless journey around the banks. With his connections she didn't doubt that he could extend the threat to every city in New Zealand...and probably Australia, too.

She shrugged as if she didn't care, her expression coolly unrevealing. 'Whatever makes you happy.'

He leaned forward so sharply that the whiskey nearly slopped out of his glass. 'You trashed my wedding without warning, without apology, without even an explanation,' he said harshly. 'What would make me *happy* is some expression of regret.'

She hesitated a fraction of a second too long and he leaned back again, his blunt features grim. 'But of course you don't regret anything, do you? Why should you? As far as you're concerned you got away with your lies.'

'I don't regret what I did,' she said bravely. 'Maybe *how* I did it, but not that it was done. Ava was my friend; I knew you weren't right for her—'

'So you *lied*. In church. In front of my family. My friends. The woman I intended to spend the rest of my life with. You said that my vows would be a lie before God but *you* were the one committing an act of desecration!'

Jane flushed and looked blindly down at her throbbing hand. She couldn't deny the searing accusation. Her guilty knowledge was a burden she would carry to her grave, and beyond—for she had not dared seek advice or absolution for her sin. She had done this man a grievous wrong in the very house of truth. Her only excuse was that he was strong and Ava was weak. He had survived—thrived, even—in the aftermath of disaster, as she had known that he would...

'You told your lies and then you disappeared before anyone could ask you for proof,' he said, with the pent-up savagery of years. 'But you knew you wouldn't need proof, didn't you? You knew that Ava was highly strung, you knew that the shock of your words would be enough to send her into hysterics. You were her best friend, she trusted you, and you used that trust to humiliate her and her parents to the extent that she never wanted to see me again.

'You were sick with jealousy of your best friend's happiness so you smashed it to smithereens by publicly announcing that you and I were lovers!'

Jane's flush deepened as she recalled the brazen words that she had flung down the aisle:

This man doesn't love this woman enough to forsake all others. He hasn't even honoured her with his faithfulness during their engagement. I'm sorry, Ava, but I can't let you do this without knowing what's been going on behind your back—Ryan and I have been having an affair for months...

'Why didn't you instantly deny it?' she choked, defending the indefensible. 'You just stood there...you didn't even try to denounce me—'

'I was as stunned as everyone else. It was such a flagrant lie I didn't think anyone would believe it for a moment...especially Ava. She knew that I loved her—'

'How can you say that?' said Jane fiercely. 'You hardly spent any time together...you certainly hardly knew her when you proposed. It was more of a business arrangement with Paul Brandon than a love-match—'

'Is that how you justified yourself?' He grated a bitter laugh and watched her flinch. 'I loved her, dammit! From the first moment we met I knew that she was the one for me...she was so beautiful, so gentle and sweet and womanly. The business deal was just the icing on the cake as far as I was concerned; my feelings for Ava were separate—private and precious.

'And that's what you just couldn't stomach, isn't it? That Ava had someone to love her and you didn't—

because you're a hard-faced, cold-hearted, selfish bitch who always has to be the centre of attention—'

'No—' Jane shook her head, a thick swath of wavy hair swirling over her shoulder, creating an inky splash against her white breast.

She didn't want to believe that he had been as deeply in love with Ava as he claimed, but, oh, God, wouldn't that explain the extraordinary viciousness with which he had come to pursue his revenge? It would also explain why he had left for Australia rather than force a confrontation when Ava had run away and shortly thereafter married someone else. If he had been in love, Ava's lack of faith in his honour would have been profoundly wounding, perhaps rendering him incapable of acting rationally in his own defence.

Based on what Ava had told her, Jane had thought it was only Ryan's pocket and his pride that would be injured if she forced the abandonment of the wedding, and those things were easily repaired for a man of his talent and toughness. But if he loved even half as passionately as he hated.

'No...' She shook away the weakening thought. If he had loved then it was an ideal, an Ava who had never really existed except in his imagination.

'Yes! So now I've decided to give you what you wanted back then, sweetheart...' The endearment was a subtle insult, an insidious threat, as he unfolded himself from his seat and loomed over her, his big fists sinking into the leather on either side of her hips, his breath hell-hot against her face.

'Tell me, Miss Sherwood, how do you like being the centre of my complete and undivided attention...?'

CHAPTER THREE

'WHERE are you taking me?'

At that moment, judging by the expression on his face, she wouldn't have put it past him to be spiriting her to some isolated spot with a quiet murder in mind.

He didn't move, still crowding her, surrounding her with the heat of his physical menace as he purred:

'Where would you like me to take you?'

Her breath caught in her throat, but he eased away and she found her wits again.

'Home, of course,' she said grittily.

Without looking away from her he sprawled back on his seat and picked up the phone at his elbow, giving the chauffeur her address. When her eyes flickered he said softly, 'Oh, yes, I know where you live… I know what you eat, what you wear, who you see. Nothing escapes me.'

'Except the occasional bride,' said Jane unwisely, wiping the smug expression from his face.

The breath hissed between his teeth. 'Ava didn't escape…I let her go.'

It was a very fine distinction, but one Jane was beginning to fear might be true.

'You had no choice,' she protested.

After fainting at the altar Ava had successfully followed her subsequent fit of hysteria with a full-blown impression of a woman on the verge of a nervous breakdown. Any suggestion of reconciliation was clearly out of the question, and her parents had been forced to bundle her away on a quiet, stress-free holiday in order that they might sweep the whole embarrassing fiasco under the carpet.

'There's always a choice. I could have proved your lie, sued you for slander, paraded the whole sordid business through the courts and the newspapers, dragged a public apology out of you—'

'Why didn't you?' She still felt a frisson of horror when she thought of all the things that could have gone wrong with her incredibly foolish plan. But she had been young enough to be fired by her own righteousness, rich enough to think that if the worst came to the worst she could buy her way out of trouble and arrogant enough to think that she was equal to anything he could throw at her...

His voice, like his cobalt stare, was riddled with contempt.

'For Ava's sake. I wasn't going to compound her hurt and humiliation by broadcasting your vitriolic lies to an even greater audience, by exposing our intimate lives in open court. Ava hated being in the public eye—even the prospect of a big wedding was an ordeal for her. Exposing her to more ridicule and gossip wouldn't have regained me her trust, or her parents' respect.'

So he had known that Ava didn't want an extravagant show on her wedding day but still hadn't supported her against her mother. Given the choice of offending her parents or riding roughshod over the wishes of the woman he loved, he had chosen the latter. What did *that* say about his so-called love?

Jane summoned her most indifferent stare as he continued savagely, 'You planned it very cunningly—I was damned whatever I did. A lie has no leg, but a scandal has wings, and no matter what penalty you were slapped with in court there would always be people who believed that there was foundation to the story. The only way to protect Ava was to remove myself from the scene. I was going to come back when the dust settled and quietly sort things out between us, but by then it was too late. Knowing how cautious she is, I certainly didn't expect her to get married on the rebound...'

'How very self-sacrificing of you,' said Jane, crushing down a pang of sympathy. At some stage everyone involved in the sorry saga had modified their actions in order to protect Ava from cruel reality, when in actual fact the helpless little darling had been a clear-eyed pragmatist, operating on her own agenda!

'A concept you wouldn't understand...not with your heritage,' he sliced back with razor-edged sharpness. 'I wonder if old Mark is looking up from his seat in hell, cursing his only child for letting the worldly goods he sold his greedy soul for slip through her fingers...'

His insulting familiarity made Jane wary, prey to the ambivalent feelings that mention of her parentage always evoked. Mark Sherwood had been as crude as he was shrewd. Not many people had liked him. 'You knew my father?'

He smiled unpleasantly. 'By reputation only. Gone but not forgotten, you might say...'

His cryptic answer implied there was a great deal more, but as she tensed Jane bumped her sore hand against her thigh and a vicious jab of pain sent a fresh wash of nausea rolling over her, exacerbated by the motion of the car as it swayed around a corner.

She tried to localise the pain by consciously relaxing the rest of her body, closing her eyes and tipping her head back against the top of the seat, unaware that her sudden physical pliancy was viewed with cynical suspicion by the man opposite—especially as the slow rotation of her tense shoulders allowed the deep bodice of her gown to dip and tighten enticingly over her ripe breasts.

His big hands clenched at his sides, his blue eyes brooding over the gypsy-dark tumble of hair and the unmistakable signs of stress in the strong-boned face, the

hollows shadowed by the thick fan of her lashes and
the new prominence of her haughty cheekbones under
the pale skin, translucent with tiredness. The lips, which
were normally barely touched with discreet colour, were
tonight a block of bright red gloss, now slightly smeared,
that revealed a surprising fullness, the lush curve of her
mouth a sensuous counterpoint to the straight, almost
masculine slash of her thick ebony eyebrows. His eyes
drifted back down to her breasts, to the long legs tilted
away from his.

'You have his looks.'

'Whose? My father's? I thought you said you didn't
know him,' Jane said, without opening her eyes. She
knew from his gravelly tone it wasn't meant to be a
compliment, even though her father had been considered
extremely handsome in his heyday. A man who was attracted to Ava's delicate, blonde, china-doll brand of
femininity was bound to find Jane less than enchanting.

'I know he was big. Dark. Chunky.'

She was in too much pain to take offence, as he
clearly intended her to do. She was big-framed but she
wasn't fat, and in the last few stressful months she had
actually dropped below optimum weight for her height.

'So are you.'

She opened her eyes and found him contemplating the
similarity with distaste, absently manipulating his
bruised jaw with his blunt fingers.

'Does it hurt?' she asked involuntarily, jerking upright
as she realised the vulnerability of her position.

'Yes,' he growled.

'Good.' There was a small silence as they measured
glances, blue on blue. 'You've still got blood on your
mouth,' she felt driven to add. 'In the corner, on the
right.'

He probed the place with his tongue. 'Sure it's not
your lipstick?' he jeered, taking the immaculately folded
white handkerchief out of his jacket pocket.

His answer caught her by surprise, and because she wasn't sure she flushed. She felt again the hard, crushing grind of his mouth, the fierce stab of his tongue impaling her senses, filling her with the angry taste of him.

He studied her hectic colour for a moment before wiping the stain from his lips with a taunting slowness. 'Better?' He held out the handkerchief. 'Your turn.'

'For what?' she said suspiciously.

'Your lipstick's smudged. It's obviously not kissproof...not that it would need to be. You usually just freeze off any man who gets within touching distance, don't you *Lady* Sherwood?'

Normally the snooty nickname didn't bother her, but this man gave it an extra bite that made her snap. 'If he's anything like you—yes!'

'You haven't dated the same man more than twice in the last two years...they can't all be like me!' he said drily.

'I've been too busy,' she replied icily, and immediately regretted it as his eyes narrowed in sly triumph.

'Have I been working you too hard? Were you afraid that I might sneak in and snatch your business while you were otherwise engaged? Too bad, since it happened anyway. Maybe you shouldn't have cold-shouldered all those likely prospects that Daddy tried to set you up with... Oh, yes, Ava told me all about them. But none of them could compete with your ambition, could they? All work and no play...no wonder Jane is such a dull, lonely girl—'

'Go to hell!' she flashed for the second time that night, aware that in her inarticulate rage she sounded more like a sulky teenager than a seasoned businesswoman renowned for her acid wit. She should be immune to his insults by now—but her sense of self-worth was badly damaged and she no longer seemed able to maintain the icy, unemotional façade that had been her vital strength during the last two years of ceaseless pressure from Spectrum Developments and its charismatic owner.

'Why, I do believe we're already there,' he murmured in mock surprise, looking out of the window as the car slowed down outside a strip of rundown wooden buildings. 'Or someplace very much like it. Parkhouse Lane is a bit of a misnomer, isn't it? I'd call it more of an alley than a lane. Quite a come-down from the Sherwood mansion. Who would have thought three years ago that Lady Jane would one day be living in a poky one-bedroomed flat above a greasy take-away joint?'

He looked at her sitting rigidly on the edge of her seat as the chauffeur turned into the kerb. 'Still, it's not as if it's for much longer, is it...? Has your landlord given you your notice yet?'

She ignored him, trying to hide her growing panic as she fumbled for the doorhandle with her uninjured hand. The letter she had received the previous day had literally been the last straw. She had figured that she had nothing left to lose from one last, futile act of defiance.

Big mistake.

Ryan Blair evidently thought otherwise.

To date their battle had been conducted publicly, their poisonous exchanges filtered through clients, employees, lawyers, banks, formal letters, contracts and writs. Personal contact had been minimal. But, having won their public war, it seemed he was now preparing to transfer the battleground to the private arena, where Jane was frighteningly vulnerable.

'I understand the poor man has been having a bit of trouble with council inspectors...something about fire regulations, I believe?' he said, catching her by the left hand as she finally got the heavy door open and attempted to slide past him to the dubious freedom of her new and soon to be former neighbourhood. Jane almost screamed at the pressure of his iron fingers, vaguely aware of the chauffeur standing by the open door, a witness to Ryan's oozing sympathy.

'That's something they're very strict about, so I suppose your landlord has told you he won't be able to give you the usual two weeks' grace to find somewhere else to live. You don't seem to be very lucky in your search for permanent accommodation since the bank sold up the old man's pride, do you? Most places you enquire about you miss out on and those you do manage to get... Well, this is—what?—the third time in just over a month that you've had to move due to unforeseen circumstances arising with landlords or flatmates—'

Jane's head whipped round, her hair swirling like a black storm around her pale face. The fact that the council inspections had been conducted on a secret tip-off and that her flat was the only one that couldn't be occupied while being brought up to 'complying standard' had clearly borne the mark of Ryan Blair's influence. But all those other times, when she had presumed she'd been simply unlucky...

Damn him!

'Are you beginning to feel you might be jinxed, Jane?' he enquired silkily. 'That maybe you're on a slippery downward slope to nowhere?' He raised her throbbing hand to within a hair's breadth of his mouth in a parody of polite salute. 'It's a long, dark, dirty, dangerous way...but perhaps someone'll catch you before you hit rock bottom. Who knows? If I'm feeling generous, it could even be me...'

Jane twisted her hand away and stumbled out of the car on unsteady heels, his dark laughter following her into the ill-lit street.

'Goodnight. Sweet dreams.'

Her dreams that night were anything but sweet. It took her ages to undress, and by the time she was ready for bed her hand was hurting so much that she had to take the last two aspirins in her medicine cabinet.

They didn't seem to help much and she tossed and turned for hours on the hard sofa-bed that had come with the partly furnished apartment, worried about the stack of bills that she could only afford to pay if she used the bond her landlord was obliged by law to return. But that would mean she wouldn't have the money to offer as bond on another flat. Even in shared accommodation one was expected to pay a lump sum up front.

Worse, her small reserve of cash was dwindling alarmingly fast, and the company was continuing to accumulate debts against her name even though it was no longer operating. Since she was directly responsible for all monies owed by Sherwood Properties, and lawyers' and accountants' fees had already eaten a huge hole in the surplus from the sale of the house and unhindered personal assets, the threat of bankruptcy loomed ever closer. Without a car it was going to take longer to get around the sprawling city, hampering her search for a job, but at least she would no longer have to contemplate skipping meals to pay for petrol!

When she finally fell into a troubled sleep Jane was tormented by lurid monsters who gnawed at her fingers, and when she woke in the morning she was horrified to find that her left hand had swollen like an overripe piece of fruit. The blade of her hand was blue and pulpy, her skin feeling as if it was stretched to bursting point and the fingers almost impossible to straighten. Moving carefully, she showered and searched her wardrobe for a dress that didn't have a back fastening.

Unfortunately there wasn't a lot of choice. Her former lifestyle had dictated very few casual clothes, and most of her custom-designed business suits and high-fashion dresses had been forfeited, along with her jewellery and extensive collection of shoes, when the bank's valuers had swept through the Sherwood residence, spiriting off everything that was considered saleable. What was left would have fitted into two suitcases—except the match-

ing leather luggage had gone too, and Jane had been
forced to leave the house with her remaining possessions
packed into plastic supermarket bags.

The black dress had fortunately been out for cleaning
at the time and the valuers had been so ruthless in the
execution of their duty that when Jane had later found
the dry-cleaning receipt in her purse she had had no
qualms about claiming it for herself. She looked on it as
a symbol of hope, a small victory over the forces of
darkness: a reminder that, even when the odds were
stacked wildly against you, you could sometimes still
win.

The black dress now hung shoulder to shoulder with
off-the-peg skirts and blouses and the subdued dresses
that the all-male valuers had considered 'of insufficient
interest' to turn the quick profit the mortgagee was demanding. At least she had got to keep all her underwear,
despite the famous French and Italian labels, but they
had only left her three pairs of shoes, all of them flats.

Jane struggled into a simple shirt-waister with large
buttons that were easy to do up one-handed and didn't
even bother trying to put up her hair.

Ever since she had moved in two weeks ago she had
walked three blocks to a tiny pavement café where, for
the price of a cup of breakfast tea, she could read the
morning newspaper and copy out all the likely prospects
from the Situations Vacant columns. Then she would
return to the flat and write her application letters before
starting the rounds of interviews and enquiries at the
various employment bureaus. But today there didn't
seem to be much point. With her hand the way it was
she wouldn't present the image of flawless competence
that she had glowingly described in her CV.

In an effort to relieve the swelling Jane tried bathing
her hand in water chilled with ice-chunks chipped off
the sides of the tiny freezer compartment of her fridge,
but although the pain was numbed for a while it only

seemed to get worse when the cold wore off, and by mid-morning she knew she was going to have to see a doctor.

When she returned the borrowed black high-heels to the girl who lived in the even pokier flat next door, Collette—she had admitted it wasn't her real name but 'guys think it's sexy'—offered some gratuitous advice.

She shook her bleached head at the sight of the mangled hand, her crystal earrings clacking with outrage. 'God, did that guy you were meeting last night do that? One of *those*, eh? Been there, done that, honey. Take my advice—dump him! And ignore any sob stuff—bastards like that never change…a few drinks and pow! They thump you and make you think it's your fault.'

Jane smiled weakly. For all his ferocious temper Ryan Blair wasn't a physically violent man. He was an expert at more sophisticated forms of intimidation…like kissing!

'You should have used the shoes,' Collette advised. 'We don't wear them just 'cos they make our legs look miles long, you know. A stiletto in the groin can give a man a whole new perspective on life, know what I mean?'

Jane nodded hastily, suspecting that the 'we' to whom Collette referred was a loose street-sisterhood engaged in a profession much more venerable than her own.

Having cheerfully targeted a few more choice portions of the male anatomy where application of a stiletto could produce instant indifference to the idea of violence and/ or sex, Collette gave Jane the address of the nearest emergency medical clinic. On the back of a dog-eared medical centre card, prominently promoting its STD clinic, she wrote down the numbers of the buses that Jane would have to catch there and back.

It was the first time Jane had been on a bus since her schooldays, but she was in too much pain to appreciate the novelty. The clinic's crowded waiting room was also a first for her, and after a long, enervating wait Jane was relieved to be ushered into a bare office where a depressingly bouncy young doctor examined her and diagnosed a broken bone before sending her off to the X-Ray department 'just to make sure I'm right'.

'What does the other guy look like?' he chirped forty-five minutes later, when Jane had come back with the X-Ray and he had clipped it to the light box to show her the thin, pale line unevenly bisecting one of the five long bones of her hand.

A fleeting vision of a dark, handsome face, inky hair and piercing blue eyes made her heart give a nervous skip. Thank goodness the doctor wasn't taking her pulse. 'I beg your pardon?'

'See this?' He tapped the image. 'You've broken the fifth metacarpal bone—the one that joins your wrist to your little finger—broken it right in the middle. Well, as far as I know there's only one way to break this particular bone like that—with a blow. *Ergo*, you hit someone or something with real enthusiasm!'

'Someone,' admitted Jane, looking at the skeleton of her hand and wondering how such a tiny fracture could cause so much pain.

'Any other injuries?'

'No—I think I just split his lip. He roared like a wounded bull so I don't think his jaw was broken or anything...'

'I mean to you,' the doctor said wryly. 'Was it your husband? What did he do?'

'Oh.' Jane flushed at his assumption. 'No, nothing like that...I mean, we hardly know each other. We're just...'

The doctor's grey eyes suddenly sparked with recognition. 'Just good friends? Hang on a minute.' He spun aside and walked over to pull a broadsheet newspaper out of the waste-paper basket beside his desk—a national daily. He leafed through the crumpled sections until he found the one he was looking for and smoothed it out.

'I thought I recognised you when you walked in.'

There were two long photographs side-by-side—one a slightly blurred shot, obviously taken the moment after impact, showing Jane's left arm at full extension and Ryan Blair, head snapped back, arms flung out, toppling across the restaurant table; the other, horribly crisp and clear, was a close-up of their seemingly steamy kiss in the street.

Some wag of a sub-editor had headlined the pictures: SHE'S A KNOCKOUT!

And the story underneath was wittily couched as a boxing match... 'Weighing-in', 'seconds out', 'round one', 'the final bell'...

Thank God the reporter obviously hadn't bothered to go very far back in the files, for it was very much a 'once-over lightly' piece, dealing only with the tail-end of the Sherwood Blair feud and too full of deliberate boxing puns to be taken seriously.

As Ryan Blair had predicted there was much sly speculation about business turning into pleasure, but there was no mention of Jane being the veiled woman who had aborted his wedding—probably thanks to the Brandons, whose damage control at the time had consisted of smothering the intriguing, 'disappearing mistress in the hat' story with urgent bulletins on the life-threatening viral infection which had caused Ava's untimely collapse and subsequent withdrawal from society for a lengthy period of convalescence.

Looking at the picture of herself wrapped in Ryan Blair's bear-like embrace, her neck arched by the apparent passion of his kiss, her half-open eyes suggesting a dreamy bliss, Jane felt an unwelcome frisson of excitement.

'Right, well...let's fix that up, shall we...?' The doctor became all efficiency again, directing her to sit on the edge of the examination table, drawing a wheeled trolley up beside him.

'Do I have to have it in plaster?' she asked, her heart sinking at the prospect.

'Nope. Not this baby.' He delicately lifted her hand. 'It's a fairly straightforward break so I'm just going to strap it to your ring finger to pull the bone straight while it heals.'

'Just strap it up?' It sounded too easy. 'For how long?'

'Probably three weeks.' He touched her little finger and she winced. 'Have you taken anything for the pain?'

'Only a couple of aspirin last night...it was all I had in the flat.'

His eyebrows rose. 'You'll definitely need something stronger than that by the time I've finished with you. You're going to have an uncomfortable few days until the local inflammation eases and the healing process starts. I'll give you an injection of local anaesthetic now and a prescription for painkillers that you can have filled at the clinic pharmacy. They're fairly strong, so don't mix them with anything else.'

The anaesthetic was fast-acting, and Jane could watch in detachment as he tucked cotton wool between her little and ring fingers and firmly strapped them together, covering the adhesive with a short crêpe bandage that encompassed her hand, leaving her thumb and other two fingers free.

'That'll protect the strapping and remind you and everyone else that you have an injury. Try to keep it dry and use the hand as little as possible. Don't drive or do anything that puts a strain on the blade of your hand— the more you promote movement in the area the longer the bone'll take to heal. And if the pain gets worse, or you're worried for any reason, come back.'

Jane frowned. Her father had been a stoic, but she was a weakling when it came to physical suffering. Perhaps it was something she had inherited from her mother, who had walked out on her husband and child when Jane was only six because—according to Mark

Sherwood—'She didn't have the guts to make a go of it. Typical woman—would rather snivel and run away than stand up for herself when the going gets tough.'

'Why should the pain get worse?' she asked the doctor warily.

'The most likely reason is because the strapping is too tight. But...sometimes, if there are complications and the bone doesn't heal properly, we might have to ask an orthopaedic surgeon to operate. But it's highly improbable in your case—unless you intend to try for another knockout!'

Jane ignored this tactless attempt at a joke and studied her hand with its bulky wrapping. 'Three weeks...' she said gloomily.

'Look on the bright side—at least it's your left hand,' he said.

Jane looked up at him. 'I'm left-handed.'

'Oh. Bad luck. What kind of work do you do?'

'At the moment, none at all.'

He quickly recovered his irritating bounce. 'Good. That's good! It means you can rest that hand—'

'It means I can starve,' she corrected him. 'If I don't find a job soon I won't be able to pay for food and rent, let alone medical bills.'

He put his hands up. 'Hey, don't shoot—this is covered by Accident Compensation; you'll hardly have anything to pay. What kind of job are you looking for? What sort of qualifications do you have?'

If Jane hadn't been tired, hungry and scraped raw by the previous night's encounter she might have been amused at being patronised by an earnest young man no older than herself who was probably scarcely out of medical school.

'Managerial,' she said tersely. 'But the sort of positions I'm interested in seem few and far between these days.'

Especially with Ryan Blair handing her the modern

equivalent of the Black Spot—a red-flagged credit-rating.

'So I've lowered my sights and lined up a few interviews for office jobs, sales, temping...the kind of thing that requires a certain manual dexterity, or at least an ability to *write*...'

'You can still use a keyboard—'

'Not very efficiently.' She shrugged. 'If I was doing the hiring *I* probably wouldn't give me a job. You don't take on someone if there's a chance they'll be applying for sick leave before they even get started!'

'What about Social Welfare; will they help?'

She sighed, beginning to think that pride was another luxury she would have to learn to do without. 'I'm involved in some heavy-duty financial wrangling...I'm not eligible for any government assistance until it's straightened out.'

'You're certainly eligible for support payments if your injury prevents you from working,' said the doctor, scribbling on his pad. 'They'll pay you a percentage of your weekly earnings averaged out over the past year. I'll get the receptionist to give you an application form before you leave...'

Jane muttered an agreement as she accepted the prescription he had scrawled out, not wanting to get into a prolonged discussion of her depressing situation. The problem was she hadn't *earned* any income in the last twelve months. So desperate had been the situation at Sherwood Properties that she had waived her salary and ploughed it back into the business, living off her various platinum credit cards in the expectation of better times ahead.

Over the next few days Jane saw several opportunities that she had managed to set up slip out of her bandaged grasp, just as she had predicted to the young doctor. She had done everything right—dressing smartly, if incredibly slowly, getting Collette to put her hair into its customary sleek roll, checking out the buses to make sure she wouldn't be late for the widely dispersed interviews and presenting a pleasant, quietly confident demeanour no matter what the provocation. From her shrewd observations two of the rejections were genuine declines, the other three were because of her identity.

On the way back to the city bus terminal one lunchtime, aware of an empty afternoon stretching ahead of her, Jane impulsively called into the first employment bureau she had registered with, and the owner—a bluff, straightforward woman whom Jane knew slightly from her former life—was quietly blunt.

'I'm telling you this, Jane, because I think it's unfair for you to waste any more of your time...but I'll deny every word I say outside this office. A bureau like mine depends on a lot of repeat business from the big companies. If we don't deliver what the clients want and cater to their every whim someone else will get the business. The truth is, if I place Jane Sherwood in a job right now I risk losing several lucrative contracts, and I'm not prepared to do that. It's probably the same at other agencies. There's a lot of influence at work. I'm afraid you're very much on your own...'

So what else is new? thought Jane that night as she decided on an omelette for dinner. The harsh reality was that she had always been more or less on her own. Even when her father had been alive their relationship had been more competitive than supportive.

A job wasn't even her top priority any more. She had to move out in three days and she still hadn't found a place to live.

There was a knock on the door and she nearly dropped an egg. It was the mousey man from the flat on the other side of Collette.

'Telephone for you.'

'Oh, thanks.' She gave him a grave smile and nipped

out into the hall, still holding the egg, to where the receiver dangled on its long grimy cord from the battered wall-phone. Eagerly she tipped the egg into the shallow cup of her bandaged hand and picked up the gently swinging receiver. 'Hello?'

'Miss Sherwood?'

Only one man said her name with that particular blend of menacing sibilance.

Jane looked down at the raw egg slithering out of its splintered shell on the top of her shoe.

'Mr Blair. What a pleasant surprise.' She, too, could be insultingly polite. 'How are you?'

'Extremely well, thank you. And you?'

Jane instinctively hid her broken hand behind her back. 'Oh, absolutely spiffing! Never been better!'

There was a small silence. Jane could hear him breathing and unconsciously regulated her own so that he wouldn't know that her heart and lungs felt as if she were running a marathon.

'I'm calling to ask whether you'd like to have dinner with me at the Lakepoint Hotel tomorrow evening? I have a business proposition I'd like to put to you, one that could be of considerable financial benefit to us both...'

CHAPTER FOUR

'AH, YES, madam, Mr Blair is already at the table—
please follow me.'

Jane nervously smoothed her palms down the side-
seams of her dress as she trailed the maître d' across the
room. The Lakepoint Hotel restaurant was justifiably famous for its elegance, and she had resigned herself to
wearing the black dress again. In her former life she
would never have dreamed of wearing a dress twice in
a row in public, and she knew that Ryan Blair, with his
ruthless eye for detail, would recognise the gown and
draw the obvious, humiliating conclusion.

However, when she had approached Collette for a second loan of her shoes, the other woman had thrown open
her bulging wardrobe as well, and Jane had been unable
to resist the opportunity to thumb her nose at her enemy
by selecting something that would bolster her bravado.

Now she was beginning to have second thoughts
about her boldness. The dark green beaded synthetic
minidress might be the current height of fashion but it
wasn't Jane's style at all; it was too trendy, too attention-
grabbing, too...*young*. Although the sleeveless scoop
neckline of the bodice was relatively modest, the
stretchy fabric hugged her full-bodied curves and revealed more of her long legs than she had displayed
since she was a teenager.

Perhaps she shouldn't have let Collette persuade her
to leave her hair loose and do her make-up, but the other
woman had been very persuasive when she realised that
Jane was meeting the man with whom she'd had her
highly-publicised fight. Collette's condescending pity

had turned to admiration when she had realised that it was Jane who'd done the hitting, rather than the other way around, but she had been highly sceptical when Jane had insisted that the new meeting was strictly for business reasons.

The maître d' rounded a bank of ferns and Jane spied a familiar dark head at a table in the centre of the room. Oh, God! Every cell in her body registered its usual instant antagonism and the apprehension that had trickled down her spine now became a raging torrent. She must have been mad to come here, to believe that Ryan Blair's tantalising hint of an end to his vendetta meant anything but trouble. Why bother to offer her a helping hand when he knew he had her on the ropes? By accepting his invitation wasn't she revealing herself as desperate enough to clutch at any straw?

Her pride balled in her throat and briefly she entertained the idea of turning tail, but then the dark head swivelled and she felt the laser-burn of his vivid blue stare. Trapped, her defiance blazed back into being. Oh, hell, who was she trying to kid? She *was* desperate enough to clutch at straws.

Fighting down her nervousness as they approached the table, Jane's fingers curled reflexively into her palms and she winced, glancing down at her left hand. Another weakness she had to hide. She had taken off the bandage and tape and tried to use make-up to conceal the mottled bruising, but the purple and yellow ripening on her skin had been too vivid and she had been forced to borrow yet another item of clothing from Collette—a pair of short black satin gloves, frilled at the wrist.

A couple of hours out of its strapping wouldn't affect the healing of her bones, she had told herself, not if she was careful to avoid putting any undue pressure on the outside of her hand. She didn't want to be accused of playing on Ryan Blair's sympathies—if he had any—

any more than she desired to see him gloat over the backfiring of her grand gesture of contempt.

There was no evidence that her blow had had any lasting effect on *him*, she noted sourly as he rose to greet her. His sculptured mouth and hard jaw were unmarred by any blemish, a testimony to his apparently unassailable physical superiority.

She noticed with a small sting of satisfaction that his blue eyes had dilated at the sight of her dress. He appeared momentarily transfixed by the beads, which were sparkling brilliantly under the light from the chandelier immediately overhead. The knowledge that she had managed to surprise him was a fillip to her battle-scarred spirits. Score one for Collette! Jane allowed herself a tiny smile of triumph as she inclined her head in a dignified greeting and sank down into the padded velvet chair drawn out by the maître d'.

'Dressing the part?' he murmured, a quizzical light entering the intense blue gaze as it returned to her face.

She tensed, sensing an insult in the cryptic, barely audible remark. 'I beg your pardon?' she said haughtily.

He sat down, smiling at her in a way that made her skin prickle all over.

'You're looking delightfully…bold and adventurous this evening,' he rephrased smoothly, signalling for drinks without taking his eyes off her wary expression.

Her thick black eyebrows lowered. 'Thank you,' she grated, the polite words simmering with resentment.

'My pleasure…Jane,' he responded, with a hard glimmer of amusement which goaded her into forgetting that she had vowed to be cool and conciliatory, no matter what the provocation.

'You're looking rather exquisite yourself, *Ryan*,' she bit back with insulting sweetness.

Unfortunately, the flattery was no more than truth. In a white linen jacket that emphasised the breadth of his shoulders, a dark blue silk shirt and black trousers, he looked the epitome of male elegance, and his blunt, handsome features, alive with the aggressive energy which infused his personality, had an impact that even Jane was unable to deny.

He knew it, too, damn him! The man oozed self-confidence as he settled back in his chair, looking even more amused at her ungracious response to his remark.

'Quite a mutual admiration society, aren't we?' he drawled. 'What would you like to drink? I'm going to have a vodka martini, with a twist.'

It was on the tip of her tongue to refuse anything alcoholic—she was going to need a completely clear head to deal with this devious swine—but his innocent question acquired the insidious flavour of a challenge as it filtered through her suspicious mind.

'I'll have the same,' she told the hovering wine waiter coolly.

'I was beginning to wonder whether you were coming,' Ryan commented as their drinks were being fetched.

She hadn't been late on purpose. A friend of Collette's had given her a lift, and the slick, streetwise young man had had a very flexible interpretation of time, but she had no intention of letting Ryan know the agonies she had gone through when she had realised that she wasn't going to arrive at the appointed time.

She lifted a taunting brow. 'Unused to being stood up?'

'Except at the altar, yes,' he replied, punishing her temerity with a bluntness that sliced through her composed front with dismaying ease.

Jane's face paled as she met the fierce blue gaze. 'You weren't...stood up,' she choked.

'No, but the result was the same, wasn't it? A bride-groom rejected at the altar...'

Jane swallowed. 'You—could have tried again—married someone else...' she said feebly. Surely a man with

Ryan Blair's raw charisma would never have to be alone—except by choice.

'And who do you think I should have taken as a substitute bride?' he sneered. 'My secret lover, perhaps?'

It was a measure of how far she was off balance that Jane was momentarily confused. 'You were having an *affair*?' she gasped in horror. It had never even occurred to her that Ava might have had genuine grounds for calling off the wedding. Oh, God, had she put herself through all this agony for *nothing*...?

'Why, yes, I thought you knew,' he purred.

Her stuttering thoughts came to a crashing halt and colour flooded back into her pale cheeks as she suddenly ralised what he had meant.

'If you think that I—that I—' She floundered, at a loss for words.

'Expected me to make an honest woman of you?' he finished helpfully. 'Well, it fits the scenario. Were you trying to provoke me into doing the honourable thing, darling? Is that why you did it?'

'*No!* Of course not,' she uttered raggedly. 'You—I — we never— Don't be disgusting.'

'You think the honourable and holy estate of marriage is disgusting?' he enquired. 'What fascinating hang-ups you have, my dear Jane.'

She felt like a moth squirming on a pin. 'I'm not your dear anything,' she said severely, grappling for her vanished poise.

'Oh, but you are.' he contradicted her, his voice silky with menace. 'You *cost* me very dear, Jane. In fact, you're the most expensive woman I've never slept with. After our non-existent affair I was left with precious little to offer any other woman... I had to fight tooth and nail to pull myself out of the financial quicksands.'

She knew it would be a waste of breath to plead that she had never intended him to be financially crippled.

'Money isn't everything. If a woman loved you—'

'Like Ava did, you mean? For richer for poorer, against lies and calumny... Oh, yes, love is the ultimate guarantor.' He laughed harshly, bitter cynicism in every line of his face.

Jane looked guiltily away but he wouldn't allow her to evade him so easily.

'What's the matter, Jane?' he asked grimly. 'Did you think I was going to let us pretend that it didn't happen? It is, after all, the reason that you're here...'

Her head snapped back. 'I'm here because you said you had a business proposition—'

'Ah, yes.' He sat back again, his smile wolfish as the drinks were set before them. 'My proposition. And you're so eager to hear it that you're prepared to dine with your worst enemy. I *am* your worst enemy, aren't I, Jane?'

He seemed to relish the idea so much that she couldn't resist puncturing his self-importance. 'I look on you as an obstacle rather than an enemy,' she said stonily.

'A toast, then.' He lifted his glass. 'To obstacles.' His eyelids drooped, giving him a deceptively sleepy, sensuous look. 'May they soon be mounted.'

'*Sur*mounted,' Jane corrected, reluctantly raising her drink.

He touched the rim of his glass delicately to hers, like the salute of a duelling foil. 'I think I prefer my version,' he murmured, and, holding her suspicious eyes with his, quaffed half his martini in a single swallow.

Distracted from his cryptic words by that smug masculine challenge, Jane followed suit, forgetting her intention to cautiously nurse her drink. The slug of potent alcohol exploded in her empty belly, making her blink, infusing her with an instant all-over warmth. The icy core of fear inside her melted a little. Hell, what more could he do to her that he hadn't done already?

'Amazing, the things that one will consider doing

when one is floundering in the murky depths of despair, isn't it, Jane?' he mused.

'What sort of things?' asked Jane warily, twisting her martini glass between the finger and thumb of her right hand, her left lying protectively in her lap.

His mouth stretched in a charming smile that didn't reach his eyes.

'Oh…the principles once ardently defended that one is prepared to compromise, the dangers ignored, the traps that one can be lured into out of the desperate need to feel back in control…'

With a jolt Jane noticed the thread-like mark bisecting his lower lip, only noticeable when the corner of his mouth tilted at that particular sardonic angle. A tiny scar, almost healed and scarcely detectable—except to the person responsible for putting it there—and the victim himself.

'I think I'm quite aware of the pitfalls of business, thank you,' she said, taking another sip of the clear, frigid liquid.

'If you were, I doubt you would find yourself in your present untenable position,' he pointed out succinctly. 'Your lack of qualifications and inexperience probably had a large part to do with your failure.'

As usual the accusation of failure hit her like a blow upon a wound. Her spine straightened. 'I might not have any formal qualifications but I had practical training that's worth any number of theoretical diplomas…nearly ten years involved in almost every aspect of Sherwood's—'

'My goodness, that long…?'

His mockery stung. How dared he dismiss her achievements so lightly? 'My father would never have allowed me to take over if he hadn't known I had the ability—'

'Since he didn't have a son, he had no choice, did

he?' Ryan interrupted. 'How that must have stuck in his craw. Mark never did have much respect for women.'

With a few brief sentences Ryan made her feel like a little girl again, desperately trying to win the unqualified approval that she knew would never be forthcoming, no matter how good, how clever, how worthy she proved herself to be.

Jane glared at him. 'I was the best *person* for the job!' she said icily. 'I knew that company inside out.'

And loved it. She had felt more at home in her cosy office than she had done in the huge, ostentatious, designer-decorated house that Mark Sherwood had built as a monument to his success. After her father's enforced retirement, work had become even more of a refuge from the tensions at home. In her office Jane had felt safe, strong, empowered by the respect accorded her position, insulated from the doubts and uncertainties that plagued her as soon as she stepped over the threshold of her father's house and faced the daily barrage of complaints and criticisms.

'If you have such a low opinion of my professional capabilities I don't understand what I'm doing here.'

'Oh, you will,' he murmured, his gaze sliding past her shoulder.

'What are you—?' She halted as he rose, his cynical expression eclipsed by a smooth smile of greeting as he held out his hand to the stocky middle-aged man with unnaturally dark hair who had come to a halt by their table.

'Hello, Dan, glad you could make it.'

'How could I have bypassed such a tempting offer?' the older man chuckled in an Australian drawl, enthusiastically pumping the outstretched hand while his spaniel-brown eyes slid sideways to Jane's startled face. 'Hello there, little lady.'

Before she could react to the patronising tone Ryan intervened suavely. ''Little'' is a definite misnomer, as

I'm sure you'll soon discover for yourself. Jane, I'd like you to meet Dan Miller. Dan owns a construction company in Queensland. He's over here to sign some contracts with Spectrum. Dan, this is Jane.'

The omission of her surname seemed vaguely insulting, but Dan Miller didn't seem to notice anything lacking in the introduction. 'Pleased to meet you, honey.'

Jane set her teeth in a smile as she found both her hands taken and squeezed. Inside her left glove Jane could feel the unknitted bones grinding against each other, and a familiar red-hot throb began to radiate through her wrist when she finally managed to extricate herself.

She barely heard the words the two men exchanged as Dan Miller eased his weight into the chair on her left. Her attention had been so focused on Ryan that she hadn't noticed the extra table-setting. Now she realised that he had never intended for them to dine alone.

'I thought this was going to be a private meeting,' she murmured in an undertone as Dan Miller turned to discuss his drink order with the waiter.

'Is that what I said?' he murmured back, eyes glinting with mockery.

'No, but that was the obvious conclusion,' she admitted stiffly.

His dark head dipped and she automatically leaned closer to hear his words. 'I try never to be obvious—it makes one predictable. And when one is predictable one is vulnerable...don't you agree?'

Was he implying that she was too easily predictable? Jane frowned, nibbling at her glossy lower lip. Her father had always accused her of being the opposite...too prone to 'womanly whims' to make logical business decisions.

'You look tense,' he continued in that same, velvety deep voice. 'Why don't you stop worrying and enjoy your meal?' he invited softly. 'One of the reasons I brought you and Dan here is because the hotel chef has a justifiably magnificent reputation, so let's not risk spoiling our appetites by conducting business on an empty stomach, hmm?'

His cobalt eyes were hypnotically persuasive. 'Relax and be sociable...Dan's an extremely valuable contact and he's only in town for the night; I'm merely asking you to help me make his evening a pleasant one. I promise you'll be amply rewarded for your efforts in keeping him entertained...'

His smooth switch in approach was bewildering. Jane had seen Ryan Blair in a number of moods but she had never before been a victim of his charm. Even knowing that it was being ruthlessly wielded in order to get his own way didn't lessen the impact.

When he had been engaged to Ava his manner towards Jane had been noticeably reserved. She had rarely seen him relaxed and he had never laughed in her presence. That must be why his sudden warm smile now made her stomach dip. His whole face shifted, the cynical lines of experience curving, softening and erasing the hint of threat in the hypnotic gaze which burned with a fierce intensity that beckoned her to fall into their fathomless blue depths. It was like looking at a different man, a stranger whom under other circumstances she might have...

Heat flushed through Jane's veins as she guiltily realised how far her mind had wandered. Steel doors slammed shut on the forbidden thoughts and she jerked back in her seat, horrified to realise how close her face had drifted to his during their whispered conversation.

What had he been saying? Something about her being sociable to his other guest. Was he suggesting that she act as his hostess for the evening? The idea was so bizarre that she shivered.

'Are you cold?' He laid a finger against her bare upper arm, and again the brief physical contact had a mind-clouding effect. Jane's mouth went dry; as she looked down she saw the fine hairs rise on her skin, all the way down to her wrist. Fear. It had to be fear creating this smothering, debilitating awareness of his physical strength, his power.

It was Dan Miller who answered, with the hearty boom that seemed to be his natural mode of expression.

'Cold? I know just the way to warm you up. How about tripping the light fantastic with me? That dance-floor is looking awfully lonesome with nobody on it!'

He grabbed Jane's left wrist and pulled her to her feet, the jolting reminder of her injury helping to startle the automatic protest out of her mouth.

'Really, I don't think—'

'Oh, go on, Jane. I don't mind being abandoned to my own devices, and you know how much you enjoy dancing,' Ryan interposed lazily as she floundered for a tactful form of excuse. 'If I get bored over here by my-self I can always come over and cut in,' he added to her dismay, and Dan laughed.

'No chance, mate!' he said, tugging Jane in his wake. 'It's your own fault for not evening up the numbers. Find your own dancing partner; I've staked my claim on this one!'

Glancing back over her shoulder, Jane saw Ryan was wearing a complacent smile of satisfaction, his half-closed eyes glittering as he watched them thread their way through the tables to the small, fan-shaped polished wooden dance-floor.

Although he was a competent enough dancer, light on his feet in spite of his stocky build, Jane found that Dan's ebullience made even a sedate waltz a challenge as he constantly sought to out-perform his own ability. On the turns he added extra steps, flourishes and dips that forced her off balance, forcing her to maintain a tight grip with her left hand that made her sore fingers feel as if they were trapped in a wringer.

Perspiration filmed her body as she mindlessly followed Dan's eccentric moves, fighting to block out the increasing pain by concentrating all her attention on his sprightly conversation. She discovered that he was staying at the hotel, he was in his early fifties and acrimoniously divorced. He chuckled over the fact that Jane was a full head taller than he was, and joked that he always felt safe in the arms of a well-built woman.

If he hadn't been hurting her she might have been amused by his heavy-handed gallantries, but as it was she merely pinned a vacuous smile to her face and endured, relieved when the set ended after the second dance and her cramped fingers could relax.

Ryan made no attempt to disguise his interest in her body as they returned to the table, his big frame lounging in his chair, his eyes studying her over the top of his glass as she walked towards him, rising slowly from her legs to the sway of her hips, to the shimmering fabric tautly encasing her generous breasts. He had got over his initial surprise at her attire, it seemed, and was now intent on a more intimate inventory.

Angry adrenalin coursed through her veins as Jane realised she was being mentally stripped by a connoisseur. She wasn't going to let him undermine her confidence in herself as a woman as well as her ability to run a company. Shoulders back, her hair flaring around them, she flaunted her last few steps with a defiance that made his eyes narrow and his chin lift sharply, the way it had when she had clipped it with her fist. As it had then, a hot wildness trembled in the air between them. Then he smiled, and Jane's skin tightened at the benign pleasantness that prowled across the primitive features.

Ryan Blair benign? Mild and gentle? She didn't think so!

As they sat down the waiter came to take their orders and Jane, who had arrived with the intention of taking full advantage of a free meal, found herself scanning the menu with a total lack of appetite. She had a feeling that if she tried to put anything deliciously rich or spicy into her tense stomach it wouldn't stay there long. In the end she chose a salad starter, with grilled fish as her main course.

'No need to stint yourself on my behalf, Jane,' Ryan said drily, in a tone that implied she was trying to impress him with the economy of her choice. 'I can afford to indulge your taste for luxury—you're not going to spend the rest of the night washing dishes in the kitchen.'

'I should say not! We have better things to do, don't we, honey?' Dan gave her an incomprehensible wink of complicity. 'Not dieting, are you, Jane? No need to with a sexy figure like yours.'

His crude flattery didn't soothe away the sting of Ryan's words. 'No, just selective,' she said, directing a blue glare at her tormentor that made him smile sardonically.

Her right shoulder kicked up and she half turned so that her hair swung forward, obscuring her face from his line of vision, attempting to ignore his taunting politeness by pretending a fascination she didn't feel for Dan's brash tales of his own numerous exploits.

To her surprise Ryan made no attempt to interrupt, allowing Dan to dominate the conversation and Jane to get away with her studied rudeness. Unfortunately she paid a painful price, for Dan liked to touch as he talked and whenever her left hand was idle he would cover it with his own, playing with her fingers, squeezing to emphasise the punchlines of his jokes.

Twice more he rousted her onto the dance-floor. After the second occasion Jane excused herself and, staring at her brittle face in the powder room mirror, knew that it was time to admit defeat—she wasn't going to be able to get through the evening without some chemical assistance. Her hand was throbbing unbearably, and the two

glasses of wine she had hoped would have an anaesthe-
tising effect had made her head begin to pound.

She was not going to give in now, dammit! Ryan had
offered a reward and she was going to hang in there until
she could demand her due: a moratorium on his revenge.

She dug into her drawstring bag for the painkiller the
clinic doctor had prescribed and dry-swallowed the
small, innocuous-looking capsule. After a moment's
pause she took another, reasoning that a double dose
would be twice as fast and effective and last twice as
long. She wasn't intending to drive or operate machin-
ery, and who knew when this interminable evening
would end? She lingered on as long as she dared in the
fashionable marble cavern, reapplying her warpaint and
brushing her hair, mentally girding herself for a fresh
round of bruising social courtesies.

The pills provided a euphoric buzz rather than the
deadening numbness that Jane had expected, and, without the pain clouding her perceptions, she suddenly became aware of the thinly veiled malice with which Ryan
was watching her try to fend off Dan's increasing over-
familiarity. It struck her forcibly that he had deliberately
needled her before Dan's unexpected arrival, guessing
that her knee-jerk reaction would be an attempt to crunch
Ryan's ego by cold-shouldering him in favour of the
brash Australian.

She tried a polite yawn and a tentative comment on
the lateness of the hour.

Ryan shot back his cuff to expose the stark Roman
numerals on his watch and observed blandly, 'Mmm, all
good girls are certainly tucked away in their cosy little
beds by now...'

'Are you implying I'm not one of them?' Jane challenged, her blue eyes turbulent with repressed aggres-
sion.

Dan chuckled, his thigh drifting suggestively against
hers under the table. 'Are you kidding? You wouldn't

be here if Ry didn't think you were very, *very* good. He told me you were class, honey, real class—and he was right!' As he groped for her hand she hurriedly wrapped it around her water-glass, and he was forced to settle for patting her knee with a moist palm.

'Oh, really, what else did he tell you about me?' Jane swiftly jerked her leg away as his touch threatened to wander, a slimy suspicion slithering around in the murky depths of her imagination.

'Well, honey, if you really want to know...why don't we go up to your room and discuss it over a nice night-cap?' Dan's slightly bloodshot brown eyes crinkled in a friendly leer that gave Jane goose-bumps. She knew what sort of nightcap he had in mind and it wasn't the alcoholic kind! Before she could summon the words to adequately voice her outrage he suddenly spotted an acquaintance at a distant table and jumped to his feet.

'Hey, Tom!' He gestured expansively with his brandy-glass, his voice booming across the elegant room. 'Fancy seeing you here. How are you, old mate?' He dropped his voice and clapped Jane on her slender shoulder, his pudgy fingers curving possessively over her bare skin.

'Gotta have a little chat to Tom—be back in a tick, honey. Why don't you settle up in the meantime, Ry? Then Jane and I can toddle off and do our own thing. Thanks for fixing it up—I'd ask you to join us for our nightcap but you know what they say...three's company and all that!'

As soon as he was out of earshot Jane leaned forward, her eyes aflame under furious black brows as she fired her suspicions point-blank at her target.

'What exactly is it that you're supposed to have "fixed up" for him?' she demanded savagely. 'What makes him think I would go anywhere with him? And how did he get the impression that I'm staying here?'

Ryan slid a flat hand towards her over the heavy white tablecloth. He lifted it to reveal a plastic key-card embossed with the Lakepoint logo. 'Perhaps because you are. In room 703, to be precise.'

'What are you talking about?' Jane whispered, staring at the key as if it were a grenade primed to explode in her face.

'Well, since he thinks you're so classy you can hardly take him back to your sleazy flea-pit,' he said contemptuously. 'And in view of his divorce proceedings he can't risk taking you to *his* room. Anyway, I thought you'd appreciate being able to conduct business on your own piece of turf, albeit a temporary one. This way you don't have to check in or out, and when your "discussion" with Dan is concluded to his satisfaction you can simply discreetly disappear.'

The key blurred as a mist of red descended across her vision, a thick, suffocating blanket of rage and soul-shattering disappointment.

'So this is your so-called *business* proposition?' she choked, almost shaking with the fury of her emotions. 'You want me to sleep with Dan as a favour to you, to sweeten some deal you have going with him? And what do I get out of it?' she spat sarcastically. 'Your gratitude and goodwill? Your agreement to stop hounding me?'

'Oh, I had a far more professional arrangement in mind,' he interrupted silkily, stroking the scar on his lip. 'I did promise you a generous reward for your co-operation, didn't I, Jane? And I *always* keep my promises...'

He reached into the pocket of his jacket and withdrew a folded piece of paper with his fingertips. Holding her eyes with his, he once again slid his hand towards her with a taunting slowness. This time, when he removed it, a cheque lay on the starched tablecloth between them. A bank cheque, Jane noticed in a single, sweeping glance. Her spine stiffened.

'Money?' Her voice dripped with disdain as she snatched it up to flaunt her scorn at his transparent attempt to humiliate her. 'You expect me to prostitute myself for the sake of—' Her eyes fell upon the amount and her icy tone cracked in disbelief at the number of zeros. 'F-for *ten thousand* dollars?'

His cobalt gaze glowed with an unholy light as he greedily drank in the disintegration of her haughty mask, his dark, slashing features acquiring the recklessness of a devil incarnate as he purred seductively, 'Tempting, isn't it, Jane? Just think—you could earn more in one night than you ever did in a month...that's if being a high-priced whore doesn't go against your precious Sherwood principles!'

CHAPTER FIVE

JANE wanted to launch herself across the table and scratch his eyes out. She wanted to kick and bite and scream bitter invective, that would condemn him to everyone within hearing as a vile and despicable monster.

The only thing that stopped her was the certainty that that was how he expected her to react. His stillness gave him away; it was that particular straining stillness of a predator gathering himself for the kill.

She could feel him willing her to lose control. He *wanted* her to throw a screaming, hysterical fit, to create another humiliating public scene that would set the seal on her already soiled reputation.

'What's the matter, Jane?' he goaded softly. 'Isn't it enough?'

They both knew it was too much—far too much. Jane would have been able to shrug off the obvious insult of a few dollars with a disdainful laugh, but this kind of serious money was enough to give anyone pause, let alone a woman who was drowning in debt. All she had to do was sacrifice her pride, her self-respect…

Never!

And he knew it! He knew that she would fling his degrading suggestion back in his teeth!

A dangerous cocktail of alcohol and drugs spiked with anger swirled stormily through Jane's veins. Colour streaked along her cheekbones, adding a fiery animation to her features as she lifted her chin and stabbed him with a poison-tipped glare.

'You think I'd fall for a con like this? What's to stop

you cancelling the cheque tomorrow—if you haven't already?'

She might have known he would provide no such easy escape from temptation. 'As you can see, it's a bank cheque, not one of my own...it's as good as cash in your hand.'

'A great deal of cash for a single transaction.' She was proud of the fact that her voice didn't falter.

'Don't you consider yourself worth it?' he asked silkily.

'Every cent,' she said, folding the cheque and meticulously creasing the edge before folding it again.

'Consider it in the light of a retainer.' His deep voice was taut with anticipation as his hooded eyes feasted on the jerky movements of her gloved fingers, waiting for her to contemptuously tear the folded square into tiny pieces. 'Naturally I'll expect to command your exclusive services. I have numerous overseas clients who like to be entertained in style while they're in town, men who prefer a more intelligent, sophisticated companion than is usually supplied by the local escort agencies...'

Jane's fingers tightened involuntarily on the cheque and she saw the infinitesimal muscular shift in Ryan's body as he braced himself for an explosion.

Instead, she tapped the slim column of paper against her lips, then smiled sweetly as she trailed it down her throat and tucked it into the scooped neck of her dress, where it nestled securely in the lacy cleavage of her bra. Then she put her elbows on the table and leaned forward to enjoy the fruits of her pre-emptive strike, laughing huskily into the congealing triumph on Ryan Blair's face.

'Why, thank you, Ryan, the money will definitely come in handy...but I hope you don't mind if I think over that exclusivity clause? I don't like to close down my options before I thoroughly investigate the market.'

For a moment he didn't move, then the full realisation

that she was calling his cruel bluff detonated in his consciousness.

'You don't mean that,' he said hoarsely, his eyes lowering to the spot where the cheque had disappeared.

'Don't I?' She flipped her hair back over her shoulder with a carelessly provocative gesture, fired with a wild glee. He was about to find out that she could bluff as well as he—and better! 'Why not? I'm desperate and, as you pointed out, desperate people take risks that they normally wouldn't even consider taking...'

His black-browed scowl betrayed his thwarted frustration. Muscles flickered in his hard jaw and she could almost hear his teeth grinding. Oh, yes, revenge was indeed sweet! thought Jane dizzily. No wonder Ryan had pursued it with such relentless fervour...

'What happened to the famed Sherwood pride?' he sneered. 'What would *Daddy* say if he knew his little girl was doing business on her back?'

Jane wondered why his insults persistently nagged on the paternal theme. Did he imagine he was trampling on sacred memories? She had no illusions about her father's business morality—and, far from being his protected 'little girl', she had been toughened fast and early by his insensitivity and rigid expectations. He had seen nothing wrong with accepting dates on Jane's behalf from men whom he shrewdly judged might be useful to him— which made Ryan's choice of humiliation rather ironic.

Maybe his taunts were more revealing of the vulnerabilities in his *own* background!

'I wonder what *your* father would say if he knew you'd turned into a pimp!' she flashed back.

Dark colour flooded his hard face. 'My father was killed twenty years ago,' he grated.

Curious at the lingering intensity of grief in his voice, Jane felt a pang of shame. 'I'm sorry...was it an accident?'

'No.' His denial held a wealth of repressed anger that sent a prickle down her spine.

'He was *murdered*?' She was jolted by the idea of anyone *daring* to deprive Ryan Blair of anything that was rightfully his. He would have been at a vulnerable age for a boy—just entering his teens. It was difficult to visualise him as a child but she imagined he had been aggressive even then, a dark, intense little boy with a fiercely possessive streak.

Jane's hand crept unconsciously to her breast, flattening over the small, prickly piece of paper that now felt the size and weight of a boulder. 'I'm sorry,' she repeated nervously as the silence stretched. 'It must have been a difficult time for you...'

Ryan's raw laugh of contempt made her regret her momentary display of compassion. Like her father, he obviously viewed it as a weakness to be turned against her.

'Still, maybe it explains what a bastard you turned out to be,' she rallied spitefully. 'Your mother obviously couldn't teach you any manners. I bet you were a hellion as a teenager.'

He bared his teeth. 'I still am, sweetheart. And let's leave my mother out of this...she's no part of our fight.'

Fortunately by this time Jane was feeling no pain whatsoever, and she was able to ignore the pressure on her injury and bat her long, mascaraed eyelashes at him, her eyes bright with reckless exhilaration.

'Are we fighting?' she said with honeyed innocence. 'I thought this was the way you always conducted your business...you know—threats, insults, physical maulings...'

His temper was momentarily leavened by a flicker of admiration at her sheer audacity.

'You want to be mauled, sweetheart, you're going the right way about it.' He lifted her hand in a parody of politeness and took a stinging nip out of her wrist, just below the ruffled edge of her glove.

'You just can't bear to lose, can you?' she hissed as a fierce tingle shot up her arm and radiated down over her breasts, drenching her with a hateful awareness. 'And stop calling me sweetheart.'

'Just getting you in the mood.' His hard glance shafted over her shoulder. 'Dan's on his way back to the table and he's the one who'll be doing the mauling. I hope you're ready to earn your money because I understand he prefers his sex rough... He may like you to be a lady at the table but it's a slut he wants in bed.'

His bluff had failed, so now he was trying to frighten her into giving his ten thousand dollars back.

'Better him than you,' she jeered, hell-bent on making him suffer before she let him off the hook.

'Then, I guess we have a deal.'

He picked up the room key and pressed it into her captive palm, folding her fingers slowly down over the rectangular piece of plastic, one by one, his blue eyes smouldering with deadly challenge.

'So be it.'

Jane's breath stopped in her throat as she realised that he wasn't going to back down. He was daring her to go through with their devil's bargain! He really didn't care about the money...he was rich enough not to miss the odd ten thousand, and had already proved that he would go to extraordinary lengths to gather her totally under his power.

Her head whirled in confusion, one certainty forming in the increasingly foggy muddle of thoughts: he was never going to give up and go away. Maybe the only way to win against him was to let him have the revenge he craved. Maybe then he would leave her alone.

But Sherwoods never gave up! Her father might not have had any principles but Jane had created a set of her own that she had sworn to live by: her word was her bond, never cheat on a deal, never betray a friend. And this man—this man was the reason she hadn't been able to live up to those high ideals. He had haunted her past and now here he was once again trying to seduce her into forgetting her principles, turning herself into a cheat and a liar. A coward.

'Well, are we going to party, honey?' Dan asked, his hand appearing over her shoulder to plonk his empty brandy-glass down on the table. He tilted the back of her chair with a suddenness that made her gasp and clutch the seat, and grinned teasingly down into her up-turned face.

Jane glanced back at Ryan, but he had swivelled away to put his signature on the bill which had been presented on a silver tray, the slashing downward strokes of his pen almost penetrating the paper. His angry profile was bleak and unrelenting.

'Sure...' Her voice seemed to come from a long, long way away as she let Dan help her to her feet. Her brain felt oddly separated from her body and her feet seemed to float above the floor as she accompanied him out of the restaurant into the thickly carpeted foyer of the hotel, conscious of Ryan prowling silently on their heels. She could feel his brooding stare pressing on her rigid back like the barrel of a gun—cold, hard and lethally unforgiving.

An icy calm settled over her. Time seemed to stretch, acquiring a dreamlike unreality as they walked past the reception desk to the bank of lifts where the two men shook hands and exchanged final pleasantries. Ryan sounded smooth and unruffled, but when Dan noticed that the receptionist was idle, and told Jane to summon the lift while he scooted over to check his messages, she discovered otherwise. She found herself abruptly backed into the nearest pillar, corralled by a solid body and big hands planted flat against the marble on either side of her shoulders.

'He's old enough to be your father—doesn't that even bother you?' Jane could feel Ryan's burning gaze raking her pale, averted face. If she moved she would have to touch him so she froze, barely breathing, hoping that passive resistance would serve where open confrontation had so miserably failed.

When she didn't answer, his voice hardened sardonically. 'The next customer mightn't be so much to your taste. What happens then, Jane? You're selling your right to say "no". What happens if I offer your services to someone who makes your skin crawl? Will you close your eyes and think of the money while some sweating pig of a man grunts and heaves between your legs?'

Jane's response to his lurid taunts was to retreat deep within herself, beyond the reach of his controlling fury.

His hands fell to his sides and he stepped back, as if suddenly contaminated by their closeness. 'You know that if you do this there'll be no going back,' he warned harshly.

'Thanks to you I have nothing to go back *to*,' she pointed out, stepping around him to smile brittly at Dan, who returned just as the lift doors opened to disgorge a group of American tourists. She slid her arm through his and tugged him inside the vacant lift, not caring that her eagerness to get away from Ryan might be interpreted as something else.

Like a sleepwalker she accompanied Dan to room 703, handing him the key-card to unlock the door and watching him prowl around, twitching the curtains and switching on the radio, turning the lights on and off until he had created the effect he wanted. He left only a small, shaded lamp burning on the long, low, polished wood dresser, and Jane was glad of the near-darkness that shrouded the other side of the room where the big double bed loomed.

The room itself was luxurious, bland, anonymous...containing nothing to jar the senses or cling in the memory, and for that she was also grateful.

She put her black drawstring bag on the spindly table by the door, but even that movement took an effort. A stunned inertia weighted the limbs that had minutes ago been floating free of gravity, and rational thought eluded her.

She had made a deal...

The thought blazed through the fog in her brain as she let Dan take her into his arms. His hands felt dry and leathery on her skin as he tugged her face down to his. His cologne was sharp and unpleasantly astringent as it mixed with the strong aroma of alcohol on his breath She turned her head so that the lips that were about to fasten on her mouth crawled moistly down her cheek instead. She had to do this, she told herself desperately. It was a matter of honour. She had to do it to prove...to prove.

She couldn't remember what she was supposed to be proving or to whom. The cloak of inertia began to slip. A vague sense of panic broke through the drug-induced lethargy and the blood thumped in her ears as she pushed frantically at Dan's chest, conscious of the bull-like strength compressed into his stocky frame.

'What? What's the matter?' Dan lifted his head, his brown eyes puzzled rather than annoyed, and Jane felt her brief burst of terror subside as he allowed her to ease away.

'Uh, there's someone at the door,' she said shakily, having realised that the source of the thumping wasn't inside her head.

Her knees almost crumbled in relief. Ryan! It had to be him! His conscience had got the better of him. In spite of his callous threats he hadn't abandoned her to her just deserts. For that she was almost prepared to forgive him!

'Oh, good, the champagne's arrived!' Dan crowed,

opening the door and beckoning the hotel waiter inside. 'I ordered it while I was down at the reception desk,' he told Jane sheepishly. 'Know how you girls like your bubbly...and flowers and chocolates—so I got some of them, too...'

Somewhere deep inside her she had been certain that Ryan would come. 'I...I have to go...to the bathroom,' she muttered from the depths of her shock, and dived through the door behind her, her hands scrabbling with the lock.

She braced herself over the marble basin, staring at her bloodless face in the mirror. Two hectic hot spots glowed on her cheekbones where Collette had applied blusher, and although her lipstick had completely worn off her lower lip was still red where she had been unconsciously worrying it with her teeth.

She looked down at her hands. Although there was no pain the left glove was beginning to strain at the seams. Soon her circulation might be affected. Better to take the gloves off now than have to have them cut off later...

She peeled back the tight satin casings, having to tug hard to free the puffy little finger of her left hand. She looked at the exposed damage with detachment, deciding that the mottled bruising wouldn't be too obvious in the subdued lighting of the next room.

The next room, where champagne and Dan Miller waited...

In other circumstances she might actually have quite liked him, Jane thought woozily. Downstairs he had been boisterous and full of brash insensitivity, but in private the rough diamond had revealed himself as something of a closet romantic. No matter what Ryan had said, she didn't believe that the older man would physically hurt her.

The knowledge gave her the courage to venture out, leaving the discarded gloves screwed up on the vanity unit.

She was grateful to discover that the curious waiter was gone, and accepted a brimming glass of champagne with fatalistic calm. No one was coming to rescue her. She would have to do it herself. Before, Dan had just been a cardboard cut-out figure in her consciousness, just a prop in her private battle with Ryan. Now he was all too real, a human being, someone who was gruffly generous and capable of being hurt...

It was all Ryan's fault!

Jane drained her glass quickly and then sat down on the edge of the bed as she found her head spinning.

'Dan...' She had something important to tell him, she knew. Something very, very important...

'Of course, my dear,' he said with exaggerated courtesy, sloppily refilling her glass before she could tell him that that wasn't what she wanted. She realised that he was none too steady on his feet, either. Although Ryan had ordered the wine that had been served with their dinner, he had drunk even more sparingly than Jane, and as a result it had been Dan who had ended up consuming most of the two bottles.

He staggered and she instinctively grabbed hold of the elbow of his jacket and pulled him safely down beside her, then bent to place her glass on the floor. The blood rushed to her head and the glass wobbled on the thick carpet, tipping over and sending ice-cold bubbles splashing over her feet. Jane squeaked, kicking off her dripping shoes, the flurry of her legs sending her toppling back on the bed, her dress riding up around her thighs.

Dan fell back beside her, the champagne bottle still clasped in his hand, and Jane let out another shriek as the golden liquid foamed out of the narrow neck onto his chest. He merely grinned at the sight of the fizzing cascade and she raised herself on her left elbow, righting the bottle and instinctively brushing at the huge wet patch that had appeared on his half-unbuttoned shirt.

'Why don't you just lick it off me, honey?' he invited

good-humouredly, his free hand sliding under her hip to roll her on top of him.

Engrossed in their damp tussle, neither of them heard anything, but suddenly the door to the room crashed open and, almost simultaneously, Jane felt herself plucked off the bed and set ungently on her feet.

'Sorry, mate—change of plan.'

Ryan Blair reached down and hauled Dan up from the bed by his soggy shirt-front, plucking the champagne out of his hand as he marched him to the door.

When Dan spluttered a protest, Ryan bent to murmur something in his ear and the older man's resistance collapsed like a pricked balloon. With a muttered goodbye in Jane's vague direction he allowed himself to be bundled into the hall, hurrying off even before the door was kicked shut with a polished heel.

Jane stared at Ryan as he leaned back against the door, shooting the privacy bolt behind him with an ominous clunk. His pale jacket seemed to glow in the dimness, warning her of the volatile energy sheathed within its smooth contours.

'Wh-what did you say to him?' she demanded defensively. 'And how did you get in?'

The door was still intact, so he couldn't have broken it down, and she was horrified by the thought that someone from Housekeeping might have glimpsed her rolling around on the bed with Dan.

He chose to answer her second question first. He tossed something with a clatter onto the table beside her evening bag. 'I booked the room, remember?'

A key. He had kept a key!

He folded his arms across his chest. 'And I told Dan that I'd regretfully just found out that you were suffering an occupational disease in its most infectious phase...'

Jane flushed with humiliation. 'Why, you—'

He kicked away from the door. 'Be careful. Be very,

very careful what you say, Jane. I'm not in the pleasantest of moods.'

She circled warily away from him. 'You never are!'

Suddenly the mental fogginess was gone, her lethargy replaced with a raging restlessness, her body taut with a fierce readiness. Everything around her came into sharp focus, colours were more vivid, sounds more penetrating. She could even hear his breathing, quick and shallow, and the whispering rasp of his clothing against his skin as he moved. If she listened carefully enough, she believed she could hear the blood pulse in his veins. Certainly she could see it throbbing heavily in his temple as he prowled closer. The shadow on his jaw seemed darker, emphasising the image of almost overpowering masculinity.

She put her hands behind her, where he wouldn't be able to see them shake.

'What are you doing here, anyway?' Her effort to sound strong and assertive came out like a sullen complaint.

He slid his jacket down his arms and threw it carelessly onto the floor. 'Ungrateful bitch!'

Her flush deepened in the knowledge that his taunt was partly justified. But did he expect a meek 'thank you' for rescuing her from a predicament that was mostly of his making? She glared at him defiantly, and was immediately punished for her sin.

'It occurred to me that I might have been a trifle hasty in employing you without any references. So I decided to conduct a personal evaluation of your services before I allowed others to avail themselves of your expertise...'

He deftly unknotted his tie and stripped it from under his collar with a slow hiss of silk that was a provocation in itself.

Jane was appalled by the little thrill of excitement that skittered along her exposed nerves.

'You really were going to do it, weren't you?' he observed with a dangerous calm, dropping the tie on top of his crumpled jacket. 'You were going to sleep with an old man for money.'

'Dan isn't old,' she muttered distractedly as she watched him reach for his cuffs. His eyes narrowed and she added quickly, 'Look, if you're calling off the deal, that's OK by me. You can have your damned money back.'

She fished in her cleavage with her good hand and to her horror came up empty. The cheque must have slipped to one side of her bra while she was trying to wrestle free of Dan.

'It's your money now,' Ryan told her, sliding his gold cuff-links into his trouser pocket as he stepped across his discarded clothes.

Jane backed away, almost tearing the delicate Italian lace as she burrowed frantically deeper. With a silent sob of relief she finally extracted the warm, crumpled cheque.

'Here, take it. I never meant to keep it, anyway,' she said, holding it out as if it were a talisman that would ward off the dark demon of her wicked imagination.

'Did you not?' It was evident from the cynical curl of his mouth that he didn't believe her. He ignored her outstretched hand, his smoky-eyed gaze roaming from her tense face to the ruffled halo of her hair, riding the waves of midnight silk down to the glittering cap-sleeve which sagged off her left shoulder, revealing the emerald-green strap of her bra.

'No!' Her sticky toes curled into the carpet at the expression on his face as he visually traced the lacy strap down over the creamy upper swell of her breast. The oxygen in the room seemed sharply depleted. Jane gulped a steadying breath, and hitched up her errant sleeve with the hand that held the cheque. 'You know damned well I was just trying to pay you back for insulting me—'

'I can think of a better way...' he murmured, his gaze shifting to centre on the rapid movements of her breasts. The flashy little number she wore suddenly felt as if it were made of transparent shrink-wrap. Never had Jane been more conscious of her overblown ripeness!

Her nerve broke as his eyes lifted back up to hers and his hands moved slowly to the collar of his shirt.

'What do you think you're doing?' she croaked as he undid the first button with unhurried fingers.

'Exactly what you think I'm doing,' he averred softly, moving down to the next button with the same tantalising deliberation, revealing a sliver of bare chest that was sculpted of pure muscle and covered with a fine dusting of dense black hair. 'What you hoped I was going to do...'

Jane was belatedly aware of the hushed isolation of the sound-proofed room, the double-locked door barred by his solid bulk. Keeping her attention fixed on Ryan, she tried to edge to her right.

'What I was *hoping* is that you were going to step aside so that I can leave—' She broke off, diving for the bathroom, but he was primed for an evasive manoeuvre, faster as well as bigger, his strong hands catching Jane by the waist, reeling her inexorably in towards him as she dug her bare heels into the carpet.

'Liar!' he accused darkly. 'This moment has been a long time coming, hasn't it, Jane? Years, in fact...'

'I don't know what you're talking about,' she panted, twisting in his grip, pushing at him with one fist, handicapped by her need to keep her left hand out of harm's way.

'The hell you don't!' Blue flame leapt in his eyes as he shifted his weight, lifting and swinging her around until her back hit the wall beside the elegant table, trapping her there with his hips while his hard hands slid down and curved over her flanks.

'It's been there between us right from the start.

Unspoken, but always *there*—this hot, itchy feeling of mutual awareness...'

'No!' He was stirring up long buried feelings that he had no right to disinter. She lashed out with her bare feet—a mistake, since it enabled him to slip sideways between her scissoring legs and push up against the centre of her body. She twisted her torso, tossing her head wildly so that her hair lashed his face, catching in the slight roughness along his shadowed chin.

'Yes! But we never allowed ourselves to scratch that particular itch, did we, Jane? We politely ignored it and that frustrated the hell out of you. You had the hots for your best friend's fiancé and because you felt guilty about it you projected the blame back onto me. *I* was the villain for being the object of your desire, for stirring up feelings that you didn't want to acknowledge...'

'You flatter yourself!' Jane choked, denying the shameful memory of her secret obsession. He couldn't know; no one had known. He was only guessing...

He leaned into her, letting her feel the thick ridge between his thighs, electrifying her with the knowledge that he was as aroused as he was angry.

'Do I? Is it flattery to feel yourself desired? Did you think I wouldn't notice the way you vibrated like a tuning fork whenever I came into range, the way you tensed whenever we brushed against each other, the exaggerated lengths you went to to avoid being left alone with me, or spending time with Ava and me as a couple? Oh, yes, you wanted me back then, Jane...I could *smell* it on you... And you still do—that's why you came here tonight flashing your long legs and big breasts in that cheap, sexy dress—'

A glorious rage ripped through her, tearing down the barriers which she had so meticulously built up against him, spilling out years of repressed passion and resentment.

'You crude, egocentric boor—' She lashed out, striking his iron shoulder with the edge of her fist, jarring her hand open so that the despised cheque dropped into the silk folds of his open shirt.

His face hardened with savage satisfaction at the betraying fierceness of her response. 'Sex *is* crude. Crude and raw and earthy. Isn't that how I make you feel?' He looked down and scooped the creased piece of paper out of his shirt, slowly rubbing it over his mouth and nostrils. 'Aah, yes...that's just the way I remember it—the unique aroma of Jane Sherwood, the ripe scent of warm, succulent breasts...'

She was suspended in shock by the sheer primitiveness of his actions as Ryan inhaled deeply, his eyelids drooping over eyes that glowed with sensual appreciation. Her breasts began to tingle as if they were being expertly fondled, and a delicious heaviness condensed in her lower belly.

'But I know you have an even headier feminine fragrance for me to breathe, don't you, sweetheart...?'

Holding her hostage with his lambent gaze, he reached down, easing his hips briefly away from hers just long enough to slip his hand under the hem of her dress, boldly cupping the cheque between her legs. Jane cried out, her eyes flying wide as he spread his fingers, smoothing out the slick paper against the fragile barrier of sheer tights and thin panties. He began to move it delicately back and forth, setting up a tantalising friction that made her head swim and her loins ache with sweet, savage yearning.

Past and present flowed together in a confusion of images. This was Ryan ravaging her senses, sacking the secrets of her soul, plundering the treasures of her closely guarded heart...

'Stop it!' she groaned, her will to resist melting away like mist in the sun as her forbidden fantasies came to life.

His triumphant laugh acknowledged the feebleness of her protest. 'Make me!'

He crushed her mouth beneath his, parting her lips and thrusting into her moist heat, his hand continuing to move between her thighs in a teasing rhythm that created a wave of exquisite sensation so intense that Jane was swept over the edge of sanity. Heat exploded throughout her body and she clutched at Ryan in a spasm of pleasure, the arm that had been pushing him away sliding around his neck, her back arching, her hips writhing uncontrollably.

Ryan lifted his head, drinking in her panting moans.

'You're wet for me already, aren't you, sweetheart?' he muttered hoarsely, scraping his fingernail along the centre of the dampened cheque, increasing the pressure of his fingers so that he could trace the length of the intimate feminine folds that were plumping out the paper. 'Wet and wild to know what I'm going to feel like pushing up inside you…whether I'm going to be as hot and hard as I am in your fantasies…'

Jane shuddered, helpless to deny the clamouring needs of her body. Nothing in her limited sexual experience had prepared her for such a violent seduction of the senses, such a ruthless gratification of her desires.

'Oh yes, baby, you're ready for it. Let me show you how much…' His fingers rotated knowingly against the tight bud of nerves that wept for release. Jane bit off a tortured gasp and his voice roughened against her throat. 'No, you don't have to hold anything back, not any more… That's right, moan for me, Jane…let me hear how I make you feel…'

She lifted her hips to help him as he hooked his fingers into the sides of her tights and pushed them roughly down her legs, along with the flimsy emerald panties that matched her bra.

'Get rid of them,' he growled as the underwear caught around her ankles, and she obeyed, kicking them away along with the cheque that curled unnoticed amongst the tangle of nylon and lace. With a savage grunt of satisfaction he drove her back against the wall again, his tongue plunging deep into her mouth in a graphic imitation of the ultimate intimacy to come. His hips rolled against hers, the blunt outline of his manhood tormenting them both with the reminder that she was now nude under her skirt.

The dark bloom on his jaw rasped like fine sandpaper against her tender cheek as Ryan angled his head to delve once more into one moist crevice of her mouth, his hands raking up her sides to tug at the tiny cap-sleeves, pulling them down her arms until the over-stretched fabric caught at her elbows.

With a last swirl of his tongue his lips broke away and he looked down at her breasts—lush, quivering mounds, almost overflowing the low-cut emerald bra.

His nostrils flared at the erotic scent and sight of her opulent curves. 'I used to wonder why you smothered yourself in those boxy power-suits. Did you think they hid the fact you had large breasts? Believe me, all it did was make me fantasise about doing this...'

He dug his fingers into the outer edges of the lace cups and peeled her out of them like firm, ripe fruit, leaving the ruffled lace straps and underwiring to form a supporting frame for her swollen fullness. Her darkly engorged nipples jutted towards him, starkly prominent against the smooth milky-white flesh. He rubbed at them with his thumbs until they grew even darker and visibly throbbed, then he weighed her generous breasts in his palms, encircling them with his fingers and massaging them with a languid milking motion that drove her wild for more.

Her hand sank into the short, spiky softness of his hair, tugging pleadingly, and he responded instantly to the silent demand, lowering his head and using long, slow strokes of his tongue to lubricate the stiff pink peaks before taking them in his mouth, nipping and sucking with a greedy enjoyment that made her ache to give him equal pleasure. She struggled impatiently to free her trapped arms and he helped her, unclasping her bra and tossing it away as her dress fell to her waist. In some vague, still functioning part of her brain she knew she couldn't manage his remaining shirt buttons one-handed, so she tore it open, uttering a husky laugh when she heard him curse.

She had never felt so free and unfettered. There was no burden of expectation hanging over her head, no pass or fail, no sense of responsibility for her reckless actions. All Ryan wanted from her was passion, and that she could provide in glorious abundance!

He shrugged out of the shirt, staring hungrily down at her enlarged breasts, still wet from his mouth, as they scraped against his bare torso. His magnificently taut chest was slick with sweat, and when she ran her hands over the velvety-soft mat of damp hair and touched the flat olive nipples Ryan's fingers dug into her thighs, grinding her against his rigid shaft as the breath came tearing out of his lungs.

'Do it! Use your tongue...suck me...I want to feel your mouth on me,' he urged thickly, and she obeyed, discovering the true extent of her own power as his big body shuddered in her arms.

His flavour was salty, tangy, exotic, and the taste of pure, unadulterated male was like another high-potency drug injected directly into her frantically pumping heart. Desire ran thick and rich through her veins as he dragged her head back for another soul-wrenching kiss.

His hands began to move up her thighs, inching the hem of her dress up over her nakedness until he was cupping her bare bottom, kneading the firm rounded globes as they clenched with the frantic seeking motions of her hips. The slip and slide of the expensive fabric of his trousers against her burning core was exciting yet unbearably frustrating, and Jane whimpered, reaching blindly for his belt.

'Wait!' he bit out against her ear. He sank to his knees and she felt the heat of his breath hazing through the soft thicket at the apex of her thighs—and then his mouth, his tongue…and the world dissolved in a mist of thick, creamy delight. Only when he had driven her to the very brink of shivering ecstasy did he rise to his feet to kiss her again, blending the erotic flavours of male and female on her tongue. Her hands slipped from the burnished steel of his shoulders to the smooth suppleness of his strong back, loving the sleek striation of muscles, the straining tension rippling beneath his burning skin.

With a swift economy of movement he pulled her bunched dress up over her head and unclipped her ruffled bra. 'Now…wrap your legs around me,' he ordered, his voice shimmering with leashed sexual force.

He was going to take her right here, standing up! Stinging curiosity whipped her excitement to new heights and Jane stroked a thigh teasingly up his powerful flank before she hooked her knee over his hip-bone. His hands curved under her bottom and splayed along the back of her thighs, hitching her higher against him as she wrapped her other leg around his waist. He threw his head back, his spine arching to support her weight as he moved in quick, rapid thrusts against her.

His chest crushed her swollen breasts as he pushed her flat against the wall so that he could free one of his hands, but instead of dealing with his zip he dipped his finger into her moist heat and stroked the tiny hood that sheathed the secret pleasure centre of her female being. Splinters of exquisite sensation radiated out from his touch and she cried out, beating helplessly on his shoulders as she realised what was happening.

'No, please—not like this—' Not alone. She didn't want to be alone. She wanted him to be part of her, filling her with his glorious strength, not dominating her with his superior self-control and leaving her feeling empty and incomplete.

'Yes, like this...' His mouth was hot on her throat as his ruthless finger brushed the tiny sheath again...back and forth, over and over, delicately spreading the pearly essence of her desire, knowing exactly where to touch and how to send the quicksilver thrills of liquid fire spilling into a raging torrent of uncontrollable bliss. She sobbed, the edges of her vision darkening as she hurtled helplessly into the unknown, towards some far-distant uncharted star, a powerful supernova that finally consumed her in a burst of brilliant light and radiant heat, leaving her weak and trembling with the rippling aftershocks of the violent implosion.

Giving her no time to recover, Ryan spun around, detaching her clinging arms and legs and tumbling her on her back across the shadowed foot of the bed. Her limp arms outflung on the royal blue bedspread, Jane lifted her head to watch with glazed eyes as he stripped off the rest of his clothes and felt in the pocket of his trousers for a condom, which he donned with a boldness that would have made her blush if she hadn't been so fascinated by the fierce urgency of his movements.

Every part of him was constructed to the same, massive scale, Jane realised with a frisson of awe, instinctively drawing her legs together. He grabbed at her slender ankles, pulling them apart as he braced his knees against the edge of the bed.

'Don't worry, nature has taken care of our proportions. You're a big girl, Jane...you'll be able to take every inch of me,' he promised in a dark throaty purr as his fingers tightened on her ankles and he lifted them, dragging her lush body towards him, his possessive gaze lowering to the dewy glistening on the layered petals of her femininity.

'You're so aroused that coming into you is going to

be like gliding between hot satin sheets…sexy, smooth
and deliciously slippery…'

He let her feet fall on either side of his thighs and
knelt forward to brace himself above her supine body on
bulging arms. Jane felt the tip of his jutting manhood
brush against her stomach, and in her violently over-
stimulated state the fleeting caress, combined with the
carnal frankness of his words, set off another series of
small explosions inside her that obliterated the vague
stirrings of caution and conscience. Her voluptuous body
undulated shamelessly on the bed, a pale splash of rose-
pink flesh against the sumptuous royal blue cover.

Her lips curved into pouting fullness as she looked
dreamily up at the man who had caused her so much
pain but was now promising her unlimited pleasure. And
she believed him—just for this one night she could have
it all…all her hurts healed, her fantasies realised and her
lonely dreams fulfilled…

The sultry self-satisfaction in her seductive smile
made Ryan stiffen, the fierce urgency of his expression
hardening, a savage suspicion that he was being manipu-
lated adding a dangerously predatory edge to his lust.
He came down on top of her with all the finesse of an
invading conqueror, carving a path deep inside her with
a single surge of his powerful hips.

The physical discomfort was momentarily intense,
swiftly superseded by the incredible sensation of herself
stretching and then tightening around the aggressive in-
vader, absorbing him impossibly deeper into her body in
a series of fluttering internal contractions that made Jane
sigh with contentment and Ryan utter a steamy curse.
He buried his face in the hot curve of her throat, his
hands contracting on her strong hips, forcing her buttocks deep into the mattress in an effort to keep her still,
but she could no more control the instinctive rotation of
her pelvis than she could the stars wheeling in the
heavens.

An orgasm hit him almost immediately, a prolonged, wild, uninhibited eruption of pure energy that stunned Jane with its primitive violence. His muscles twisted and corded, locking and unlocking in pulsing spasms that sculpted his body into straining contortions as he bucked and shuddered, lashing himself into a frenzy in his mindless quest for climatic satisfaction. He reared up on both hands for one last, huge, hammering thrust, his head thrown back, his arched body utterly rigid, quivering like a tightly drawn bow until he let out a hoarse shout of scorching triumph and slumped down onto her heaving bosom.

Jane felt used and bruised and dazzled by his splendour. No other man had succeeded in making her feel so wildly desirable. She wasn't the sort of woman who drove men crazy. She had only had one other lover in her life, and James had turned out to be a set-up of her father's, more interested in grooming himself as a potential heir-in-law than satisfying her as a woman. For James, extended foreplay had been an irksome waste of time, and with his brisk efficiency he had ensured that Jane felt inadequate if she couldn't keep up with him.

Ryan's lax body eased off her, and Jane, suddenly self-conscious in her nudity, rolled away from him onto her side. His strong arm hooked around her waist, hauling her back against his sweaty chest as he mistook her movement for an attempt to leave.

'Where do you think you're going?' he demanded, sinking his teeth deep into the rounded curve of her shoulder, his hand cupping one soft-tipped breast. 'I haven't finished with you yet...'

He tightened his arm, turning her onto her back, anchoring her there with one hairy leg crooked across her abdomen. 'The room is booked for the whole night, my sweet little swindler. You've only just *begun* to earn your money...'

CHAPTER SIX

JANE bent down to pick up a small pebble from the firm black sand. She brushed away the clumps of clinging grains and rubbed the flat, round stone between her finger and thumb in tactile appreciation of the smoothly polished surface. She curled her forefinger around the outside edge and looked out at the wide expanse of sea. There was a stiff wind and the turn of the tide had made the early-morning surf wild, the breakers thundering to shore in broken lines, salt spray hanging like white mist over the long, flat beach.

Jane waded into the foam at the edge of the water and paused, judging her moment, then splashed sideways in a series of little hops to skim the stone into the shallows over the top of a disintegrating wave. It skipped three times on the swirling water before smashing into the next curling breaker. Not bad considering that conditions were so poor and she was using her right arm!

She backed out of the water, brushing at the splashes on her white cotton shorts. Five was still her best score. When she got the proper use of her left hand back, in a few more weeks, she hoped to be able to double it.

The wind stung her wet legs and she tucked her taped hand into the pocket of her thin wind-cheater and turned back, deciding it was time for breakfast. Trudging into the soft sand above the high-tide mark, she glanced to her left where the huge, crouching hulk of Lion Rock which separated the broad iron-sands of North Piha from the main Piha beach was obscured in low cloud and spray. By mid-morning the cloud would probably burn off and it would be another brilliant west coast summer day.

Yesterday had been a scorcher, and the usual rash of weekend day-trippers had created havoc for the dedicated surf lifesavers who patrolled the crowded main beach, but early on a weekday morning, during school term, it was only the locals, and the serious surfers and body-boarders who braved the notorious Piha rips.

She lifted her eyes from the fine black sand sifting through her bare toes to the steep, bush-clad hills above the beach. They were the western fringe of the Waitakere Ranges, which protected the fiercely independent coastal community of Piha from the brash encroachments of the sprawling suburbs of Auckland, forty kilometres to the east. There was only one dead-end road winding through the ranges into Piha, and the locals liked it that way.

There were no commercial developments in the small, isolated settlement, no shops other than a single general store, a dairy and a takeaway bar on the beachfront, and no hotels, bars or restaurants—only private residences and holiday homes, most of them owned by the same families for generations, and a council-run camping ground offering basic facilities to those wanting to pitch tents and park caravans. The core population of permanent residents was small enough to be friendly, large enough to blend into, and eccentric enough to be tolerant of a range of alternative lifestyles.

It was the perfect bolt-hole.

Jane scrambled up the tussock-seeded dunes which crested the narrow tar-sealed road that ran along the back of the North Piha beach and came into sight of her own, private bolt-hole.

It wasn't a very pretty sight. Like many of the old-fashioned holiday baches at Piha, it was a box-like rectangle of painted fibrolight panels, with extensions randomly tacked on over the years to cope with the ebb and flow of family numbers. This one was a particularly ugly faded yellow, with a red corrugated iron roof urgently in need of patching.

The paint on both roof and walls was cracked and peeling, sandblasted completely bare in places by decades of savage Piha winter westerlies. Several windows were cracked in their badly warped frames and the front door listed drunkenly on its hinges. The detached wooden garage was in even worse condition, rotten timbers proof of years of neglect, and the chain-link fence sagging around the perimeter completed the general picture of sad dilapidation.

But at least it was a roof over her head, albeit a rather leaky one, thought Jane ruefully as she pushed open the rusty gate. It was also rent-free and, most important of all, it was well out of Ryan Blair's dangerous orbit!

Her enemy.

Her lover.

She didn't know which one she feared more.

She still couldn't quite believe that she had managed to escape him. After all her previous struggles it had seemed almost too easy. Or was she only free because Ryan had decided to let her go?

The question tormented her, as did her distressingly vivid memories of the scandalous night as his sexual play-thing. She could conveniently blame the pills and alcohol for initiating her outrageous behaviour, but she had a sneaking suspicion that they were the tools with which she had subconsciously sought to lower her inhibitions to the point where she could act on her desires without feeling guilty afterwards.

If so, it hadn't worked!

The first thing she had been aware of when she had woken the next morning had been the pulsating throb of her left hand. The pain had been as bad as in the first few days after the injury. Had she rolled on it in the night? Why hadn't her fingers been safely taped up?

Her heavy eyelids had fluttered open and she'd

frowned for an instant of total bewilderment at the morning sunlight streaking across an unfamiliar ceiling. Her mouth had tasted dry and cottony, her head had felt oddly achy, and so had...

Oh, God! Through the pain it hit her: where she was, what she was doing there...

Her heart jerked in fright as she turned her head, but she was alone in the wide disordered bed, her long black hair streaming across the indentation in the pillow beside hers. Alone and naked under the white cotton sheet, her body feeling bruised and tender in all sorts of incredibly intimate places.

And no wonder! She snatched the sheet to her throat, a burning blush enveloping her as splintered images of wild, passionate excess danced in her head. What had begun as a primitive act of possession had very quickly become a prolonged orgy of mutual self-indulgence, shorn of any pretence of reluctance on either side. Ryan had seemed possessed of a superhuman stamina and an infinite capacity for invention that had shocked Jane to the core, even as she had boldly responded to the irresistible challenge of proving that she was more than a match for his devastating expertise. She had done things for him, to him and with him that she had never dreamed of doing with any man, let alone with Ryan Blair!

She was suddenly conscious of the open curtains flooding bright, white light across a tangle of male and female clothes on the floor, and the sound of running water shutting off behind the closed bathroom door. Panic surged to a peak. Oh, God, maybe she could sneak out of the room while he was in the bathroom? She rose on her elbows, but even that slight movement made her hand throb sickeningly and she sank down on the pillows again, groaning at the sight of her freshly swollen fingers.

She let the back of her fiery hand rest very gently down on the cool sheet beside her pillow. The painkillers

had worn off with a vengeance and she realised how
foolish and downright dangerous it had been to take double the prescribed amount. Not only had she risked an
overdose, but she had masked the warning signs that
might have told her she was doing more damage to her
hand.

Oh, yes, she had been a complete and utter fool all
round! Jane flung her other arm over her eyes to block
out the harsh light of day. In the condition that she was
in it would take an age for her to dress herself again.
Unless she wanted to scuttle out of the hotel wrapped in
a sheet there was no avoiding the impending confrontation. She groaned again, furious with herself for being
so weak and pathetic.

'If you're feeling stiff and sore I suggest you try a hot
shower,' came a darkly mocking drawl from the bathroom doorway. 'It's worked wonders for me...'

Jane tensed, instantly defensive, and fought a fresh
stirring of pain that wasn't entirely physical. She didn't
want to look at him but she couldn't resist a peek from
under the shadow of her arm.

Thankfully Ryan had knotted a white hotel towel
around his hips, although it rode low enough for her to
see the black, curling hair thickening at the base of his
hard belly. His tanned skin was glossed by beads of
water, indicating that he hadn't bothered to dry himself
before leaving the bathroom. His wet hair was spikily
uncombed and without a razor his chin was blue-black
with heavy regrowth.

He looked thoroughly tough and disreputable as he
sauntered towards the bed, and Jane stifled another groan
of mingled pain and self-disgust, her arm clamping back
down over her eyes.

The bed depressed heavily beside her and she felt the
heat of his hard thigh settle against her sheet-covered
hip. 'You may as well come out from hiding, Jane,' he

said drily. 'I'm not going to conveniently fade away just because you refuse to look at me.'

She bit her lip, clinging to the illusion of privacy as she felt him pick up a lock of her long, wavy hair and begin to play with it. God, when she thought of the way she had reacted to him during the night! After that first, frenzied explosion Ryan had turned out the light, and in the fevered darkness it had been all too easy to relinquish what remained of her inhibitions. No wonder he wanted to gloat!

'Jane?' He tugged on her hair and his impatience became tinged with malice as she continued to shelter under her concealing arm. 'I can't believe a woman who brazenly sells her sexual favours is shy, so perhaps this provocative pose is supposed to tempt me into doing this...'

She felt a light twitch at the top of the sheet and whipped her elbow down to anchor it in place, exposing herself to the penetrating blue gaze that she had been trying so hard to avoid.

His hard mouth curved with satisfaction. 'Good morning,' he murmured, with a pointed politeness. Her hair was a gypsy tumble and most of her make-up had worn off, the smudged remains of her eyeshadow and mascara giving her eyes a sunken look of sleepy sensuality that was much sexier than the artificial gloss of the night before.

His eyebrows rose as she failed to respond and he bent over to brush his lips teasingly against her sealed mouth, bracing his hands on the pillow on either side of her head. He was almost leaning on her swollen hand, half concealed by the overhang of the pillowcase, and Jane's whole body clenched in terror at the idea of more pain. His expression darkened as he took in her tight-lipped pallor and an angry pulse created a tic at his temple.

'Regrets, Jane?' His eyes skimmed down her tented body and back up to her frozen face. 'I'm afraid it's too late for those. I told you there would be no going back. You made your bed last night and now you're lying in it.' He staked another claim with his mouth, an insolent kiss of ownership.

'And you can take that martyred expression off your face, because we both know it's a damned lie—a woman doesn't have screaming multiple orgasms unless she's enjoying herself. At least you can stop worrying whether I'm going to ask for a refund. You were the consummate professional, darling—worth every cent!' He sat back, flicking his hands off the pillow with a careless motion that knocked against her hidden wrist.

Jane's eyes dilated in their smudged sockets and the blood seemed to rush away from the surface of her skin, leaving it icy cold...except for her hand, which felt as if it were being pierced by white-hot needles. Physical pain became indistinguishable from mental anguish, and a choking moan slipped past her clenched teeth. But not the tears; she would fight the tears until her last breath!

'Dammit, Jane, don't think you can soften me up by—' Ryan broke off, frowning as he saw the glitter at the corner of her eyes. His eyes shifted and he blanched, leaning forward to draw the edge of the pillow back from her crabbed hand. He swallowed. 'My, God, Jane—did *I* do that?' he said in a devastated whisper. 'Your finger—it looks as if it's dislocated...'

He tentatively touched the shiny, swollen skin and Jane let out another explosive whimper. He snatched his finger back as she drew her hand to her chest and hunched around it like a wounded animal.

'I know I was rough with you last night but I know my own strength—I didn't think I was actually hurting you,' he said shakenly, his face twisting into a rictus of self-disgust. 'For God's sake, why didn't you tell me? I can't believe I could hurt you that much without realising it—'

Considering how mercilessly he had tried to hurt her

in every other conceivable way it was strange that he should react with such intense revulsion at the idea of causing her physical harm, Jane thought miserably, but there was no mistaking that his horror was genuine. His peculiar sense of honour at work…

It was tempting—very, very tempting—to torture him with a lie but, unfortunately, she was in too much pain to spare the energy to torment anyone else.

'You didn't,' she gritted.

'I didn't?' The thin white line around his mouth relaxed as he took another look. 'No, of course not—the bruising is too advanced for this to have happened in the last few hours. But if it was like this last night— I might have overlooked it because the lighting in here bruised everything with shadows, but I certainly would have noticed at the dinner table—'

He stopped, his eyes jerking to her bloodless face. 'Except that you were wearing gloves…' he said slowly. 'I thought it was odd, but then your whole outfit was bizarrely out of character and it threw me off. Was that the plan, Jane? Did you hide this from me because you were afraid to let me see that you were weak and wounded?'

He saw too much. He always had. 'I'm not weak,' she mumbled hopelessly, in no fit state for another bout of verbal fencing.

'No, you're stupidly self-willed and too stubborn for your own good.' He picked up the cordless telephone by the bed.

'What are you doing?'

'I don't know when it happened or how, but that hand obviously needs medical attention,' he said grimly, punching in a set of numbers.

'It's *had* medical attention,' she cried. 'I'm not stupid—' Her father had called her that, whenever she'd proposed an idea that went against his wishes.

He ignored her. 'Carl? Ryan—I need your help.' He

rose to his feet and paced across the room to scoop up his clothes.

Jane rolled carefully onto her side, fulminating against the pain as she strained to hear his low-voiced conversation. 'What are you doing? I told you, I don't need a doctor—' Her mouth snapped shut as Ryan casually shed his towel, tucking the phone into his neck so that he could continue to talk as he stepped into a pair of thin white bikini briefs. His buttocks were as hard and muscular as the rest of him, flexing as he bent, revealing the fine dusting of hair that disappeared into the intriguing crease between his legs. He turned to face her as he pulled up his trousers, affording her a brief glimpse of the silky pouch cupping his bulging manhood.

He punched off the phone and dropped it back onto the table, shouldering into his blue shirt.

'I have a doctor. I'm not going to see another one—'

'You don't have to go anywhere. He's coming to see you.'

'The hotel doctor?' She was horrified. The management would slap on a surcharge. And weren't large hotels hotbeds of gossip? If it became known she had spent a night at a hotel with Ryan Blair her life would become even more of a scandal than it was already. Jane gingerly put a foot to the floor, trying to cradle her hand and still maintain a grip on her modesty.

'No. Mine. Dr Graham Frey. You'll find he's extremely competent...and discreet.'

'You called your own doctor?' Her agitation increased as she watched him bundle up her clothes and place them on the chair behind him, out of reach. 'I won't see him!'

Ten minutes later her blustering had weakened to a sullen whine and she was still crouched on the edge of the bed clutching the sheet around her. And he'd called *her* stubborn!

'At least let me put on my clothes—'

'For goodness' sake, he's a doctor. He's used to seeing naked women—'

For some reason that made her blush. 'If he comes in and sees me like this with you here, he'll think…he'll think—'

'That we've just spent a night of hot and heavy sex?'

She closed her eyes to shut out his mocking truth.

'If he sees you in that trashy little evening number at seven o'clock in the morning he's going to come to the same conclusion anyway,' he pointed out in an aggravatingly reasonable voice. 'There's a hotel bathrobe in the wardrobe; how about you put that on for now?'

She wearily accepted the grudging concession, and when he brought it over she was forced to let him help her slide her arms into the long sleeves. Surprisingly, he made no sarcastic comments as she scrabbled to keep the sheet between them until she was completely covered by the robe. With the towelling safely belted around her, Jane decided she badly needed a shower, which led to another battle, interrupted by a knock on the door that made Jane stiffen in alarm. Surely it was too soon for the doctor? She caught Ryan's solid forearm as he swung away.

'If it's Dan, I don't want to see him—'

'Are you pleading for my protection, Jane?'

She let go of his arm like a hot coal and scowled at him. To her shock he grinned, a sheet-lightning flicker of pure humour that illuminated his rakish features, making them look unbelievably boyish and innocent as he strolled to the door, buttoning up his shirt. There was a murmured conversation just out of her sight, and when he came back he was carrying a tray of covered silver dishes.

'What's that?'

'Breakfast. I ordered it earlier.' He set the tray down on the small desk on the other side of the bed and lifted off the silver covers, revealing bowls of cereal and fresh fruit, a rack of wholewheat toast and a cafetière of coffee.

'I'm not hungry,' she said truculently.

'No, but I am,' he said, sitting at the desk and draping a starched napkin across his knee. 'I have a full day's work ahead of me.'

And she didn't. Trust him to rub it in! Jane drew in her lower lip, feeling the hot pressure build up behind her eyes as he ate in silence. She could feel him watching her and tried to arrange her face into the familiar pattern of haughty indifference, but somehow the old tricks just wouldn't work any more. She was sick of being brave. She was sick of pretending she was something she wasn't. Who was she fooling but herself, anyway?

The arrival of Dr Frey in an elegant grey suit was as embarrassing as Jane had expected it to be, not least because he didn't arrive alone. He was preceded by a familiar lithe fair-haired man who prowled into the room with a panther-like grace, making a quick survey of the exits as he handed Ryan a small black suitcase. It was the same silver-eyed man who had been at Ryan's side when she had thrown her punch—the one who had opened the restaurant door for her afterwards.

His eyes widened when he saw Jane sitting in the bed and she lifted her chin as Ryan casually introduced his personal advisor. He didn't say what sort of advice Carl Trevor specialised in, and she quailed inwardly as the astute silver-grey eyes moved thoughtfully from her swollen hand to his employer's solid chin.

'Mr Trevor,' she acknowledged repressively, hoping to nip any open speculation in the bud.

'Call me Carl,' he said easily, undiscouraged by her formality. He came closer and nodded towards her hand with a charming smile of sympathy. 'That looks like a pretty painful injury, Miss Sherwood, no wonder Ryan

was concerned.' The smile became more personal as he
added in a soft murmur, 'Metacarpal, is it?'

Jane flushed, but before she could summon a reply
Ryan cut in and shunted his advisor towards the door
with an impatient frown. 'Thanks, Carl, but I think the
doctor and I can handle things from here...'

'Shall I wait for you outside?'

The bland enquiry earned him another darkling look.
'I have my own car here so there's no need for you to
hang around unnecessarily. I don't know how long this
might take, so why don't you go on to the office and let
Irene know I might be late in this morning. Get her to
rearrange the early part of my schedule.'

He tossed several more pithy instructions into his advisor's increasingly amused face before firmly shutting
him out and striding back to hover over the grey-haired
doctor, who had drawn up a chair beside the bed and
had begun his gentle examination.

Jane fought back the waves of pain, answering his
quiet questions about her previous medical treatment
with a reluctance which was justified when Ryan exploded, 'Broken! Then why aren't you wearing a
damned cast? What in the hell kind of witch-doctor did
you go to? Dammit, Graham, she shouldn't be in this
much pain, should she? Why don't you do something
about it?'

Dr Frey was obviously a friend as well as a physician,
for he ignored the arrogant outburst, focusing his beetle-
browed attention on Jane as he meticulously went over
the treatment she had received and sternly chided her for
removing the strapping before the bones had begun to
knit. It was apparent that he assumed that vanity had
been the reason for her actions and Jane was happy to
let his misapprehension stand.

'And the accident occurred...how?' he enquired delicately, when he had elicited the date of her injury and
subsequent visit to the clinic. From his tone she could

tell that he had drawn the same conclusion as the doctor
in the clinic. She wasn't going to be able to get away
with claiming she had got it caught in a door.

'It wasn't exactly an accident,' she muttered warily,
having seen Ryan stiffen into alertness when she had
mentioned his birthday. He was now fingering the scar
on his lip, and she decided that it was pointless to pre-
varicate any longer. 'I—I hit someone,' she sighed.

'Oh?'

'Yes. Me!' Ryan announced tightly. He looked furious
at being made to feel guilty. 'She underestimated my
hard-headedness, didn't you, Jane? A big failing of
yours—underestimating your opponents...'

'I still knocked you flat on your back,' she flared.

'Yes, but at what cost?'

'It was worth it!'

The doctor cleared his throat and opened his cavern-
ous black leather bag. Jane blinked rapidly, telling herself that the tears in her eyes were because of the pain.
Ryan swore under his breath and moodily poured himself another coffee.

'I'll retape your hand but I want you to strictly follow
orders this time, or you're going to end up needing that
surgery your doctor warned you about,' Dr Frey in-
structed Jane gravely. 'As it is, this renewed inflammation is going to set back your recovery. So from now
on, Miss Sherwood, please leave the doctoring to the
experts.'

In spite of Dr Frey's ultra-gentle touch, by the time
her hand had been rewrapped Jane was in real tears, and
Ryan was ominously controlled as the doctor took his
leave.

'Don't worry, Graham, I'll make sure she doesn't behave so irresponsibly in future...'

Jane just had time to surreptitiously scrub at her eyes
with the corner of the sheet before he swooped back,

planting himself down on the bed and caging her against the pillows with his strong arms.

'You shouldn't have implied you have any control over my behaviour,' she began, with a pathetic attempt at her former haughtiness. 'I'm perfectly capable of looking after myself—'

'You can say that? After last night?' Ryan said, piercing her with a look that made her flush and clutch the gaping neck of the oversized robe. 'Why? Why go to such lengths to hide it from me?' He laughed grimly. 'No, don't bother to answer, I think I know. Did you hear what Graham said? You could have caused permanent nerve damage—and all because of your damned inflexible Sherwood pride! Your father never taught you to recognise your own limitations, did he, Jane? You'd rather cripple yourself than admit to a simple case of human weakness!'

He ran a hand through his damp spiky hair and down over the back of his skull, shaking his head incredulously. 'I still can't believe you took such a risk. What in God's name *possessed* you?'

'Obviously *you* did!' Her acid retort was flung at him without thinking, and they both froze as the literal truth of her heedless statement sank in.

'I—I didn't mean—' Jane began to inch backwards against the pillows as Ryan lowering his arm, studying her with eyes that transmuted from angry blue to a sensuous blue-black.

She was breathing in light, quick gasps, high colour back in her pale cheeks, her thick black eyebrows clashing in defiance of the secret excitement glimmering in her wide-eyed gaze. The throbbing in her left hand had dimmed to an extent that she was reawakened to the numerous other, more pleasurable aches in her body, the subtle reminders of how thoroughly she had enjoyed his possession.

'So I did,' he murmured softly, towering over her.

'And what's done is done, isn't it, Jane? I can't very well *un*possess you...'

He cupped her chin and brushed a thumb over the dampness in the shadowed hollow under her eye.

'And nor, I think, would you want me to,' he added huskily. Although there was a masculine smugness to his certainty, it wasn't the offensive, gloating triumph of an enemy over a vanquished foe, and Jane's heart fluttered in her chest.

'I—'

His thumb flirted over her patrician cheekbone to slant across her trembling mouth. 'Don't! Don't lie, Jane. Let there at least be honesty between us about *this*...'

He bent and replaced his thumb with his mouth. He kissed her, not voraciously, devouringly, as he had kissed her all through the night, but softly, sweetly, seductively...almost forgivingly. A morning kiss, full of such delicate promise that Jane was bewitched with a bewildered yearning. She felt his hand slide under the lapel of her robe and shape her warm breast, gently exploring the stiffening peak. She might have found the strength to defy his passion, but against his tenderness she had no defences. No man had ever considered her worthy of tenderness.

'Oh, yes, it was good for both of us, wasn't it, sweetheart?' he whispered, sipping at her lips. 'Spectacularly good. So why should we fight it? Maybe it's time to stop looking back and start looking forward...'

'To what?' she asked, her mind blurred by the addictive sweetness of kisses that were far more potent than any drug.

'To what we can do for each other.' His voice lightened to a sexy, teasing drawl. 'After all, I did promise the doctor I'd look after you...'

Years of self-denial prompted her instinctive reaction. 'I don't need—'

'Of course you do—we all do at some time in our

lives,' he told her, lifting his hand from her breast to comb the tumbled waves off her smooth brow, arranging them in a dark frame around her serious face. 'And you're more needy than most, sweetheart...or you wouldn't have been so quick to sell yourself last night.'

A scalding sense of shame swept over her. She wanted to tell him that he had paid a great deal too dear for what had been given freely, but that would give far too much away. 'It wasn't like that—I was angry—'

'I know, so was I,' he soothed her, with a honeyed understanding that was even more seductive than his kisses. 'Because all the time we were mouthing insults at each other I was imagining what it would be like to have you beneath me in bed.' He stilled her restless movement by weaving his fingers into her hair, trapping her head on the pillow.

'Do you think I haven't realised that you only took the money for spite? You've got far too much pride to play the whore for me or any other man. You went off with Dan because I'd pushed you too far and you wanted to twist a knife in my guts, and things got out of hand...' His mouth twisted into a cynical line. 'But that's OK. I know how these things can happen. I'm intimately acquainted with the subtle ways that revenge can suborn the soul...'

His cobalt eyes seemed to blaze with an inward fire as he gently manoeuvred her forearm so that her injured hand lay across his large, flat palm.

'I have a serviced apartment on the beach at Mission Bay,' he said quietly. 'Small but with all the built-in luxuries you could ask for, and very private...no one need know where you are, if you want to handle it that way. If you like you could move in today.'

It took her a moment to work out what he was saying. 'Are you asking me to *live* with you?' she croaked.

'I don't live there; I have a house of my own. The

apartment would be yours,' he corrected her scrupulously, 'for the duration.'

For the duration?

'But I'd visit as often as was agreeable to both of us, and probably stay overnight fairly regularly, so naturally I'd take care of all your living expenses,' he clarified.

But Jane was still grappling with his original statement.

For the duration? He was talking about the duration of an *affair*!

Her pulse went wild. 'You want me to be your *mistress*?' she gasped.

He shot her a reproving look through thick, dark lashes. 'That's a very old-fashioned term. I have in mind a more modern partnership, one of mutual pleasure and mutual independence.'

'More modern, maybe, but no more equal,' she said shakily, while inside elation soared above her shock. So he didn't just want a torrid sexual fling—he was laying down the parameters of a *relationship*. And, typically for a dominant male, he expected it to be all on his own terms. She strove to feel insulted by his offer. 'I wouldn't exactly be as independent as you, would I? Not if I'm living in *your* flat on *your* money...'

His eyes glinted. As an experienced negotiator he was a skilled interpreter of the nuances of language and behaviour. Alert for the slightest hint of complicity, he noted that Jane's use of the present tense altered her answer from rejection to mere objection. Neither had he missed the tiny flare of her nostrils, nor the uneven rise and fall of her magnificent breasts. The lady was definitely intrigued by the bait. It only remained to reel her in.

His fingers curled lightly round her bandaged hand, caging it without pressure. 'If you still want to get a job after your hand heals, that's up to you—I'm sure you'll no longer have trouble finding one. I just want you to know that there's no need to worry about how you're going to survive in the meantime, or to fear any reprisals, whatever happens between us.'

'What are you saying?' she whispered, afraid to believe the message implicit in his words.

He shrugged with quiet resignation. 'I'm calling off the dogs, Jane.'

Instead of relief she felt a gush of pure, unadulterated terror. To believe she would have to trust him without reservation...

'Why?' She pushed him away, scrambling off the bed in a flurry of towelling, and this time he made no effort to stop her. 'Why now? If this is another one of your mind games...' she faltered to a halt, wrapping her arms around her waist to stop them reaching out to temptation.

He spread his hands in a gesture of surrender as he slowly rose to his feet. 'No games. Just the truth—that we make good enemies but even better lovers. And one night of hot-blooded passion hasn't doused the flames, has it, Jane? Until this thing burns itself out neither of us is going to get any peace.'

She could tell him that it was never going to burn itself out—not for her. 'And then what? Then we become enemies again?'

His face was sombre, moody. 'No, that's over. You won't get Sherwood's back, but I won't pursue the debts any further.'

He crossed to the black case that Carl Trevor had left and opened it, taking out a cordless electric razor and a clean shirt. Looking at his broad, unrevealing back, Jane was struck with a sudden burst of insight.

'I could never quite work out why you came after me the way you did. Even considering what I'd done, it seemed like overkill... You didn't just want to ruin me, you seemed to want to obliterate my identity.'

She moved until she could see his tense profile. 'But it was never just me, was it?' she said, slowly feeling her way with every word. 'There was something else, something to do with my being a Sherwood. You always made my surname sound like an insult. It was my father, wasn't it...?' She wondered why she hadn't made the connection before—perhaps she hadn't wanted to compete yet again with the memory of her parent. 'You knew my father—'

'And to know him was to hate him?' he interrupted, with a cool amusement that only strengthened her suspicions.

'*Did* you hate him? Why? What did he do?'

He crossed to the mirror over the dressing table and switched on the razor. 'Leave it, Jane.'

'No, I won't.' She followed him and stayed his hand before it reached his chin, meeting his gaze steadily in the mirror. 'You asked for honesty from me, Ryan...don't I get any in return? Are you going to make me find out for myself?'

His eyelids drooped and his voice took on a husky intonation. 'Do you know, that's the first time you've used my name this morning? Last night you couldn't seem to stop yourself saying it...'

She almost wavered. 'Don't change the subject.'

His mouth thinned. 'He's dead. It's nothing to do with us anymore. Whatever he did, it's over and done with—'

'He was dead yesterday, too, but it still mattered to you then,' she persisted over the burr of the razor. 'Why won't you tell me? Do you think I'd be shocked? I wouldn't. I know what kind of man my father was...'

'He was like a Rottweiler when he scented blood. He sank his teeth in and never let go.' Ryan sighed and clicked off the razor as he turned around. 'Rather like you.'

The comparison cut her to the quick, and Jane lifted an imperious chin in a characteristic attempt to hide the hurt, but before she could dredge up a defensive reply he touched her cheek in a tacit apology.

'I suppose his tenacity was the one thing I admired about him,' he said ruefully. 'All right, Jane, I suppose I owe it to you to tell you what you want to know—after you've dressed.'

He tunnelled his fingers under her hair and guided her into a kiss that warmed the chill of loneliness from her soul. His mouth was aggressive, but contained none of the repressed anger of the previous night, just a hunger he made no attempt to conceal. 'I have to leave for the office soon and I need to make some phone calls first, so let me shave and make my calls and then we'll talk...'

Jane stood on the porch of her dilapidated little beach house and watched the wind-tossed seagulls ride the swirling air currents in the sky above Lion Rock. If she hadn't been so greedy for the poisonous fruit of knowledge maybe she would still be in Auckland, living in the hope that Ryan's caring would one day become much more than casual...

But that was purely wishful thinking. The twenty-year-old scar that she had ripped open when she had sabotaged Ryan's wedding could never be fully healed. To Ryan, she would always be the daughter of the man who had murdered his father.

Oh, Mark Sherwood hadn't wielded a knife or a gun, but the impact of his actions on his victim had been ultimately just as fatal as a killing blow.

True to her word, Jane hadn't been shocked by the tale of a crooked home-building deal which Mark Sherwood had set up two decades before; she knew all too well that her father had had little respect for the law where it interfered with his own interests and protected 'fools and losers'.

By his definition Charles Blair would have been a loser, even though as a carpenter and builder he had built up a respectable business, because Ryan's father had been too honest to take his profits and run when the deal had inevitably collapsed. Instead he had tried to honour the promises he had made. As a result he had been bankrupted, and his reputation and means of livelihood destroyed when rumours that he had been using substandard building materials began to circulate. In desperation he had naïvely confronted Mark Sherwood, pleading for help, and Jane's father had laughed in his face, threatening to produce documentary evidence that it was Charles's embezzling that had caused the scheme to fail.

Charles Blair had died not long afterwards, electrocuted in his home workshop, and rumours of suicide had thrown further shadows over his blackened reputation. His pregnant wife and thirteen-year-old son had been left homeless and destitute after the debts that he had assumed responsibility for had been paid.

While Mark Sherwood had gone on to build a financial empire on his ill-gotten gains, Charles's widow had been trapped in a cycle of poverty, supporting her son and new baby daughter in a hand-to-mouth existence, taking menial positions because of her lack of qualifications and often working two jobs to make ends meet. She was now remarried, but for fourteen years she had struggled alone, haunted by her husband's undeserved legacy of shame, watching her son grow from a secure little boy into an angry young man who had sworn that one day he would be rich and powerful enough to destroy the company that had been built on the ruins of his father's honour.

But by the time Ryan had amassed a sufficient fortune and manoeuvred himself into a position to put his vengeful plan into action Mark Sherwood had been a dying man, no longer at the helm of Sherwood Properties. Unwilling to cause the innocent to suffer for someone else's crimes, as he and his family had unjustly suffered, Ryan had reluctantly curbed his lust for revenge...until

Jane had proved herself as treacherous, deceitful and lacking in moral conscience as her father.

Jane shivered as the breeze whipped across the porch and she turned to enter the shabby kitchen.

She had never had a chance. As soon as Ryan had been once more in a position to attack he had done so without hesitation and without mercy—and who could blame him?

Not Jane.

That was why she couldn't believe that Ryan really wanted her in his life, except as the crowning achievement of his search for natural justice. Maybe it wasn't even conscious. Maybe he genuinely thought that the attraction that had flared between them was worth burying his resentment to explore. But Jane didn't flatter herself that she was so special that he could be persuaded to permanently relinquish the jealously guarded bitterness that had shaped his ambition.

No, it was more likely that by making her his mistress he would be completing his revenge. He couldn't make Mark Sherwood suffer, but he could spit on his grave by stamping both his company and his daughter as his own personal possessions.

Jane had spent too much of her girlhood loving a man who had been incapable of appreciating the preciousness of her gift. She had no intention of wasting her adulthood in the same way.

So, like the coward that she was, she had let Ryan leave the hotel that morning confident of his impression that she would fall in with his arrangements. Then, sitting on the unmade hotel bed in her tacky green dress, she had picked up the telephone and reluctantly called Ava.

And, to her surprise, found her secret bolt-hole.

CHAPTER SEVEN

FOR breakfast Jane boiled herself an egg obligingly laid by one of the clutch of bantam hens that scratched a living in the bach's huge back yard and set the kettle on top of the wood-burning stove. As she ate at the scrubbed kitchen table she inhaled the rich, yeasty scent of baking bread that swelled out of the oven.

In two short weeks she had come to greatly appreciate the simple pleasures of life, just as she had begun to enjoy the challenge of bringing domestic order to the chaos that had greeted her on arrival.

Ava, who had inherited the run-down property only a few weeks previously on the death of a curmudgeonly great-aunt, had told Jane that she could have the place as long as she needed it. She had warned her that a real-estate agent had told them they wouldn't be able to rent the house out anyway, until it was cleaned up and repaired, so that the living might be rough, but Jane had grabbed at the chance to do something useful in her self-imposed exile, offering to earn her keep by giving the place a thorough clean-out and making a list of the maintenance work that was beyond the capabilities of her limited handyman skills.

Not that she needed to earn her keep, for Ava had insisted that she and her husband already owed Jane more than they could ever repay. She had been understandably shocked by Jane's telephone call begging for help in finding an inexpensive place to hide, for she had had no idea that her friend's recent business problems had become so extreme, nor that they were directly related to Ryan Blair.

Ava and Conrad Martin had moved to Wellington shortly after their wedding, and their decision to settle a comfortable few hundred kilometres away from Ava's interfering parents had enabled Jane to make light of the catastrophic impact that Ryan's return to Auckland had had on her life. She had seen no point in upsetting Ava when there was nothing that she could do to help.

Conrad, who was a mechanic looking to own his own workshop, was too proud—or too wise—to accept financial assistance from his in-laws, so the couple, already with two young children to support, were in no position to rush to Jane's aid either physically or financially. And, anyway, Jane had promised herself three years ago that she would never raise the spectre of the past as a test of their continuing friendship.

Making that phone call was the hardest thing that she had ever done, but fortunately, and somewhat unexpectedly, Ava had risen magnificently to the occasion. She had instantly acceded to Jane's strained plea that she ask no questions—even though she had obviously been bursting with curiosity—so Jane didn't have to tell any awkward lies. To admit that she had become enmeshed in Ryan's vengeful toils was one thing; to confess that she had also slept with Ava's former fiancé was quite another!

Even more fortunately, it turned out that Ava's great-aunt Gertrude had harboured a distrust of authority, and had held gloomy opinions about the fate of civilisation that had turned her into something of a survivalist. Every bit of storage space in her house had been crammed with hoarded groceries and bulk supplies and there was a huge rambling vegetable patch which, along with the hens and fruit trees, supplied most of Jane's dietary requirements.

All she required to complete her self-sufficiency was a cow, thought Jane with a wry grin as she poured some of the hot water from the kettle over the dishes in a plastic bowl and the rest into a teapot. Milk and butter were the only staples she had to buy.

Of course there were drawbacks to the simple life, especially to someone who had to cope with the inconveniences one-handed. Thankfully Ava had arranged for a relative of Conrad's to give Jane and her cartons and plastic bags of possessions a lift out to Piha in his van, but once there she was effectively stranded by her need to eke out her funds for an indefinite period.

There was an infrequent bus service to Auckland, but so far she hadn't had to use it, and although the house was wired for electricity there was no phone, and Jane was minimising power bills by using the tilly lamps and candles that Great-Aunt Gertrude had stored in generous quantities.

She had also turned off the hot-water cylinder, heating washing-up water on the wood stove in which she burned the rubbish she was gradually cleaning out of the crammed rooms and blessing the balmy summer as she took refreshingly cold showers. All Piha residences relied on tank water, so she was also careful to economise on her water usage, recycling washing water on the vegetable patch and placing a brick in the toilet cistern.

At least she had one source of help to hand. Her present reading material was a number of battered 'do-it-yourself' books and old-fashioned housewifely tomes that she had found in a dusty carton under one of the sagging beds.

Hence her fledgling bread-making skills. Jane glanced at the clock on the kitchen mantelpiece and decided it was time to see if she had yet conquered the problem of iron crusts. She opened the oven door and used a quilted oven-cloth to lift out the heavy loaf tin she had put in to bake while she went for her usual morning walk along the beach. Setting it carefully down on the work-scarred table, she pressed her finger into the raised crust, smiling at its springiness. Not perfect, but since she had been at Piha Jane had stopped trying to live up to impossible standards. She had even discovered that failing could be fun if you were willing to laugh at your mistakes instead of punishing yourself for them.

'So this is your "better offer"!'

Jane whirled, bumping the table with her hip, knocking the bread flying. Instinctively she reached out with her good hand to catch the tin before it hit the floor and spilled its contents, gaping at the man who filled the narrow doorway. Her confusion was such that it was several moments before she responded to the pain receptors screaming for attention. She yelped and threw the loaf back down on the table, gazing down at her seared palm in macabre fascination as a blister began to bubble up from the abused flesh.

'What have you done?' Ryan was by her side, his hand clamping on her wrist as he spun her over to the sink and turned on the cold tap, holding her hand steady under the gentle stream of water as he pushed in the plug.

He made her stand there with her hand in the sinkful of water while he fetched the cellphone from his car and made a call to Dr Frey.

'Yes. Yes, she does, doesn't she? No, no skin broken—blisters, though, on her palm and the pads of her fingers. Yes. Fine—I can do that. Yes, yes I will. Thanks Graham—just add it to my bill.'

As he flipped his portable phone closed and tucked it into the back pocket of his jeans Jane, still leaning over the sink, said weakly, 'You didn't have to do that.'

He should have looked less intimidating in casual clothes than he did in a suit, but somehow they just made him look tougher.

'You should know by now that I never do anything because I *have* to,' he told her. 'How's it feeling?'

She grimaced. 'Not too bad.' It was only a half-lie—

the cold water was having an anaesthetic effect on the fierce stinging. 'What did he say?'

'That there might be some psychological reason you're so accident-prone around me.'

Jane swung to face him, sending splashes across the white polo shirt he wore under an unzipped navy cotton jacket. 'I am not! It was your fault. You shouldn't have crept up on me!'

'That's right, blame someone else for the trouble you're in.' He dunked her hand back in the water. 'You need to keep it there for at least ten minutes to draw the heat out of the skin and ease the pain. Where's your first-aid kit?'

'I—I suppose there must be one around here some-where,' she said vaguely, fighting to think of something other than the solid warmth of his body as it had pressed against her spine. Why did he have to arrive when she was in shorts and a T-shirt with her hair scraped into a childish pony-tail?

'You mean you don't know?' Ryan's gaze swept dis-approvingly around the cluttered kitchen, noting the holes in the discoloured linoleum floor and the crack in the window. His mouth thinned. 'I've got one in the boot of the car. And here—sit down before you fall down!'

He pushed one of the stout kitchen chairs up against the back of her knees and waited until she had slumped down on it before he slammed out of the door.

Jane's eyes began to sting in sympathy with the raw, stinging redness of her right hand. She had learned the value of a good cry since she had been down at Piha. There had been no need to keep a stiff upper lip when there had been no one around to jeer at her tears, so she had shamelessly indulged herself. In just two weeks she had cried out years of repressed emotion. The sense of release had been enormous and now she was finding it difficult to stuff all those wayward feelings back into the tight little box of self-control where they had always belonged.

She was shivering when Ryan got back, and without a word he disappeared into the back rooms. He was gone for a few minutes and she could hear him poking around the chaos before he returned with a blanket which he tucked around her shoulders and over her bare knees. He made her try and take her hand out of the water several times before she could do so without an increase in pain. Then he sat her at the table and carefully dried off the affected area with sterile swabs and applied a large, dry non-stick dressing which he covered with a thick pad of cotton wool before bandaging it firmly.

'You should have been a doctor,' she joked into the thick silence as her slender hand was turned into an unwieldy fin. This was the second time he had handled her wounded person with a gentleness that belied his intimidating size and ruthless demeanour. In spite of the violence Ryan had brought into her life it wasn't difficult to visualise him in the role of healer.

He flashed her an unsmiling look. 'I wanted to be, but we couldn't have afforded what it would have cost to send me to med school. I went into the building sector because I needed to get a full paying job to help Mum out. She tried to be tough but she had health problems, and working at more than one job became too much for her. I didn't do a formal apprenticeship because the wages were too low, but I learnt enough about all aspects of the building business to know a good deal when I saw one.'

'Oh.' So, he had become a successful, self-made tycoon, but it was because of her father that he hadn't been able to pursue his original dream. That made two of them.

'I wanted to become a dress designer,' she blurted out, and immediately felt stupid. There was no comparison between being thwarted of entering a noble profession and one based on the frivolities of fashion.

To her surprise he didn't scoff. He glanced at her freshly scrubbed face, her plainness emphasised by the pale mouth and dragged back hair, the frowning expression. 'So why didn't you?'

She shrugged and looked away from the fingers securing the bandage, ignoring a faint ringing in her ears. She had excelled at design classes at high school but had dropped them because of her father's scorn of 'soft' subjects. Her artistic imagination had been stifled by years of trying to live up to what was expected of her, rather than asking herself what *she* wanted. But here at Piha the old, creative impulses had begun to stir again.

'Because you didn't have the guts to go against your father's wishes in case he disinherited you?' Ryan supplied when she didn't answer.

He was still kneeling by the chair, in the perfect position to see the flaring temper in her blue eyes before she abruptly doused it. 'Yes, I suppose that was it,' she said, her voice tight with the effort of not defending herself.

'Or was he withholding something else you wanted even more?' he asked softly, refusing to allow her to close herself off from him. 'Like love... Was Jane Sherwood a poor little rich girl desperately trying to earn Daddy's love...?' His jeering grin burrowed under her control. 'Or should I say a poor *big* rich girl...?'

'Oh, shut up!' she snarled, embarrassed at the pathetic picture of herself he had sketched. That might have been her at sixteen, but at twenty-six she had a lot more confidence in herself.

'Whatever else I might have wanted to do, I was damned good at managing Sherwood's. It would have been a good career for me if you hadn't come along and bulldozed it!'

He got up. 'That's better. You were looking a little

pale and shocky there for a moment. We'd better get some fluids into you.'

Jane watched him pour the tea, moving about the kitchen as if it was his own, and suddenly remembered what she would have preferred to forget.

'How did you find me?'

He spooned several sugars into her cup, ignoring her protest that she didn't like sweetened tea.

'You made a toll call from the hotel room just after I left. It conveniently appeared on the printout that accompanied the receipt they posted me—time, duration and the number that you called. Certainly it proved more informative than that polite little note you sent to my office thanking me for my generosity but saying you preferred to accept another offer.'

Jane put a bandaged hand over her mouth. She had forgotten about payment for the long-distance call. 'Oh, God—you phoned the number—'

'I find it astonishing that you've remained such good friends with the woman you humiliated and lied to at the altar, but then, as Ava said herself, she has a very forgiving nature. A pity she didn't exhibit that forgiving side of herself where *I* was concerned...'

He set the tea before her and poured a sugarless cup for himself as he sat down opposite. 'She said you were more like sisters than friends, and sisters stick together even through the bad times—that once she knew the truth she accepted that you believed you were protecting her. Quite from what, she didn't explain, but then she wasn't very coherent...'

Jane's hand fell to the base of her throat in a classic gesture of shocked dismay. Poor Ava, she must have nearly had heart failure when she picked up the phone! And no wonder, if Ryan had wrapped his questions in those dark tones of silken suspicion.

'What did you say to her?' she asked hoarsely.

'You hadn't told her very much in that one phone call,

had you, Jane?' he said with an infuriatingly unrevealing smile. 'Rather ironic, isn't it? First you lie to her about us being lovers when we're not, and then you lie to her by not telling her we're lovers when we are. Who were you supposed to be protecting this time?'

'She wouldn't have just *told* you where I was—' choked Jane, fighting a sense of betrayal. She had impressed on Ava that no one was to know her whereabouts, just in case Ryan had been lying about calling off the dogs. Maybe she should have told her friend more, but she hadn't really expected Ryan to personally hunt her down, not after she had scrawled that brief message to him on hotel notepaper, posting it on her way back to her flat in a taxi for which he himself had prepaid.

'Not during our first conversation, no. But I can be irritatingly persistent, and extremely persuasive...'

Jane had a sudden mental image of some of the more erotic methods of persuasion he had used on her in that hotel room and scowled.

'Fortunately you don't have a phone down here,' he added purringly. 'Otherwise I'm sure she'd have rung to warn you she'd let the cat out of the bag.'

More likely it had been scared out! 'If you bullied or threatened her—' she began shakily.

'What?' Ryan put his cup down, leaning his forearms on the table. 'What will you do about it if I did? What *can* you do?'

Exactly nothing and they both knew it. 'I'd think of something,' she said darkly.

'You could try,' he said amicably. 'But you needn't worry. Ava's a lot less fragile than she used to be. As it happened we ended up having a full and frank discussion that proved enlightening on both sides...'

Jane's heartbeat accelerated. 'How full and frank? Did she tell you about Conrad?'

She knew immediately that she had made a mistake.

His eyes narrowed. 'How frank do you think she *should* have been? And what about Conrad?'

'I mean…that it was—well, it was sort of Conrad's idea to let me have a go at doing this place up for them to sell while I was here,' she improvised hurriedly.

It had been foolish to think that after all this time Ava might have felt impelled into a spur-of-the-moment confession that she and Conrad had fallen in love during the last few months of her engagement to Ryan. That was why Ava had pleaded so hard for Jane's help the day before the wedding.

Ava and Conrad, her parents' former chauffeur, had finally stopped fighting their feelings and admitted their love for each other. If Jane hadn't found a way to stop the wedding then Conrad would have stepped in and done so, but, having met the quiet, lanky young man with his shy smile, gentle way of talking and fear that he wasn't good enough for the girl he loved, Jane had known that Ava was right when she'd sobbed that her parents and Ryan would make mincemeat out of him.

Jane would have had to be iron-hearted to resist the appeal of the star-crossed lovers, though if truth be told, she had also been angry with them for the hurt they were about to inflict in grabbing at their own happiness at the expense of others', a resentment that had been inextricably mixed up with her angry defiance of her own emotions.

'Oh, really?'

She realised that while she had been brooding Ryan had been feeding his suspicion by watching the rapidly changing expressions on her face.

'Why did you come?' she asked abruptly.

He raised an eyebrow. 'Maybe to find out what you did with my ten grand—the cheque hasn't been cashed yet.'

Trust him to have found out!

'Only because I haven't been able to get to a bank,'

lied Jane, her blue eyes stormy. 'I told you you weren't going to get it back. As you were so kind to point out at the time, I earned every cent of that money.'

She had intended to hold a ceremonial burning, but somehow she hadn't been able to bring herself to destroy what was the only physical evidence of their explosive night of passion. The cheque lay carefully folded in her otherwise almost empty wallet, a tribute to the triumph of pride over practicality. It also served as a concrete reminder of the futility of the treacherous, happy-ever-after fantasies that lurked deep in her soul.

'So you did,' he admitted blandly. 'I just thought you might have since misplaced it, that's all.'

He knew she had no intention of cashing it! Immediately Jane decided to do so at the first opportunity. But she wouldn't do anything selfishly sensible with it, like reduce some of her debts. No, she would take his damned money and secretly donate the whole lot to a charity devoted to fighting the oppression of women! Let him stew over what she had done with it!

'Because if you have I could always write you another.'

Realising that he was winding her up, Jane turned her attention belatedly to her cooling tea, only to discover that she had trouble picking it up. The taped fingers of her left hand hurt when she tried to lift the cup by the handle, and if she cradled it in both hands her burned right palm was seared by the heated china in spite of the thick cotton wool padding. With some juggling she managed to balance the bottom of the cup in her left palm, keeping it straight with the guidance of her bandaged hand while she lifted it to her mouth.

'Going to be difficult, isn't it?'

'What is?' she said, afraid to put the cup down again in case she spilled the contents. She hastily drank some more, pulling a face at the syrupy sweetness.

'Surviving. I guess it was tough enough doing things

with one hand, but Graham says it will be several days before that burn starts to heal. Meantime the dressing has to be changed each day and kept clean and dry so infection doesn't set in if the blisters burst. You can hardly even hold a cup of tea straight; how are you going to cook, or wash, or clean...in fact do anything around the house?'

'I can manage,' she claimed, infuriated by his logic. He was so smug and male, so...*whole*.

'But why should you have to?' he said smoothly. 'After all, as you pointed out, it's my fault you're in this state, and I did promise Ava I'd make sure you were OK. She was most concerned to learn that you'd come down here with a broken hand. You didn't tell her *that*, either...'

Her cup crashed down sloppily in its saucer. 'Damn you, she hadn't seen the newspapers—I didn't want to go into all that—'

'Neither did I, so I didn't tell her you'd broken it on my face! Didn't you believe me when I said I was calling it quits? When you come back to Auckland you'll find I've already spread the word that you and I have settled whatever differences we had.'

Jane looked down at her hands as the realisation that had been slowly building over the past two weeks burst, fully-formed, upon her consciousness. She didn't *want* to go back. Ryan's act of revenge had inadvertently given her the chance to start life completely afresh. Yes, she was afraid of her uncertain future, but she was also exhilarated by her freedom. Cut adrift from the stresses and expectations of the past, she could shape her own destiny. She didn't *ever* want to go back to being the person she had been—obsessed with success and maintaining control, lonely, driven, profoundly unfulfilled...

She drew in a deep breath. 'Look, I don't know why you bothered to follow me down here—'

'Don't you?' He moved around the table. 'You think

I should have accepted your insultingly brief note as the last word on the matter? If you were serious about giving me the kiss-off the least you could have done was to give it to me in person!'

At the mention of kissing her eyes moved helplessly to his mouth and flickered away, but he had seen the brief flash of hunger.

His voice deepened with predatory shrewdness. 'Or maybe you just didn't trust yourself to be able to say no to me face to face. Afraid your desires might slip the leash again, Jane, and that we'd end up back in bed together? Is that what sent you scuttling down here?'

As usual he made her uncomfortably aware of the conflict in her behaviour. *Had* she been subconsciously delivering a challenge when she had run away? Jane crossed her arms over her chest, shaking her head sharply again, but this time Ryan reached out and caught her pony-tail as it flipped past her ear, winding the silky black skein around his hand, forcing her head to a stop. With his other hand he tipped up her chin.

'Coward!' he taunted.

For once she didn't rise to his bait. 'Is it so impossible for you to believe that I'm just not interested?' she asked steadily.

'Not impossible...' He dragged his thumb suggestively across her lower lip and watched her eyes dilate and her breasts tremble with a ragged inhalation. 'Just highly unlikely.'

And before she could argue with the breathtaking arrogance of that he added quietly, 'Given our history, maybe you're right to be afraid...but why let the past deny us a chance to explore the unique pleasure that we give each other? Why not let something good come out of the bad, get it out of both our systems...?'

His thumb rubbed at her mouth. 'You're a city girl. You don't have to live like this—you don't *belong* out here. Come back with me and I'll provide you with as much challenge and excitement as you can handle. We both know from bitter experience there are no guarantees in life, but one thing I can promise is that I'll do nothing more to deliberately hurt you...'

She believed in the sincerity of his words but the promise rang hollow in her heart.

No, Ryan might never hurt her deliberately, but he would hurt her all the same. It was as inevitable as the tide rolling up Piha beach each day that if they became lovers Jane would be the one to suffer most from a break-up. If anything, she felt even *less* equipped to handle an affair than she had been two weeks ago. This time alone had stripped from her the hard shell of sophistication that she had always worked so hard to maintain.

Becoming Ryan's lover might temporarily satisfy the yearning of her body but it would only intensify the craving in her soul. He was like an escalating addiction, and the only safe way to escape before she was totally hooked was to give him up cold turkey.

'Good, you'll turn around and leave, then,' she said stonily. 'Because it so happens that I actually *like* living "like this".' She jerked her pony-tail out of his grip with a fierceness that made her eyes brighten with tears, waving her bandaged hands vaguely in the air. 'I don't want to leave Piha and I certainly don't want to get involved in an affair with anyone at the moment! I just want to be left alone. Is that clear enough for you?'

She was devastated when he didn't even try to argue. He merely gave her a hard, all-encompassing look, a grim nod and strode out of the house. She watched his powerful car spitting angry stones from the tyres as he turned on the gravel shoulder of the road outside her gate and roared out of her life. Then she sat back down at the table and sobbed her heart out.

Mopping up, she told herself that his giving up so easily had proved her doubts about any relationship they might have had. He couldn't have wanted her so badly after all. His ego had demanded he track her down but when he found her in her unkempt surroundings looking plain and scruffy, an object of pity rather than lust, he had realised that she was no longer a challenge to either his intellect or libido.

All morning, as she doggedly struggled against her new handicap, she told herself that she was better off without him. She would survive this as she had survived every other setback in her life—alone.

Several hours later she was out in the back garden, tired and sweaty, hunting along the hedge for more eggs, when she thought she heard a strange noise in the house. She put her basket down and moved around the side of the garage, frowning at the sight of a white panel van parked on the sun-burned grass of her front yard, a telephone company logo emblazoned on its side. She walked around the front just in time to see a man in white overalls disappearing through the open front door.

'Hey!' Jane shouted, and ran after him, nearly tripping over a woman in the same telephone company overalls who was crouched in the narrow hall, drilling into the chipped skirting board. 'Hey, what's going on here?'

'Hooking you up for phone and fax,' said the woman, around several screws clenched in her teeth. 'Your connection to the house checks out OK, but some of this cabling has to be upgraded.'

'You must have the wrong place. I didn't order anything. You've got to stop!' When the woman didn't take any notice Jane gritted her teeth. She still hadn't got used to the fact that people no longer jumped to comply when she gave orders. 'Who's in charge here?'

The woman jerked her cropped blonde head in the direction of the living room where the man had gone, and Jane hurried to confront the culprit. He was setting up a top-of-the-range fax in the corner on an old kauri desk that Jane had devoted her evenings to restoring, scrubbing away the grime of years and rebuilding a fine

patina with oil and beeswax. He was young, and aggravatingly unconcerned by her protests.

'Look, there's obviously been some mistake—' If Ava
was desperate to warn her that Ryan had discovered her
whereabouts she might have ordered a phone, but no
way would she have bothered with a fax, let alone such
an extravagant model. 'Have you got a worksheet with
you?' she demanded. 'I want to know who ordered these
things—'

'I did.'

For the second time that day Jane nearly suffered a
heart attack at the sudden appearance of Ryan, striding
into the room carrying a large suitcase and a laptop computer. He glanced into the largest and sunniest of the
bedrooms, which she had commandeered as her own,
and walked into the next one. He set his things down on
the faded carpet square next to the heavy oak bed.

'I need the phone and a separate fax line if I'm to
keep in touch with my office. Fortunately, these days I
don't need to be there in person to run things. I can
access Spectrum's mainframe from my laptop and I've
got plenty of highly competent deputies willing to handle the meetings in my absence. With fax and e-mail I
can have their reports sooner than I would have had the
hard copy delivered to my desk.'

He made it sound as if he was moving in! 'Wh-what
are you talking about?'

Jane followed, still spluttering, as Ryan calmly skirted
the worker in the hall and went back outside to a vehicle
parked out of sight on the other side of the panel van—
not the sleek Mercedes that he had departed in earlier,
but a rugged four-wheel drive that looked well-used but
well-cared-for. He placed a hand-tooled boot on the
lower rung of the rear bull bars and reached in to haul
out another case. Standing behind him Jane was treated
to a close-up of faded denim whitening across taut mas-

culine buttocks. He turned and caught her looking, and gave her a smile that made her scalp tingle.

'Did you think I'd run away with my tail between my legs, Jane?' She flushed at the sexual connotation of his words and he uttered a gravelly laugh that suggested he had noticed her pink eyelids. 'Serves you right. But actions speak louder than words, especially to a bull-headed woman like you. Like it or not, you need help right now, and if the mountain won't come to Mohammed...'

She was still arguing with him when the two greatly intrigued telephone workers tested their state-of-the-art communications system and reluctantly left.

'You can't just move in on me like this.'

'I already have,' said Ryan. Having ordered his possessions to his liking, he stretched out on the bed he had chosen for his own, grimacing at the dust that rose and the sag in the middle of the creaking old wire weave that barely supported the mattress. 'Is yours any better than this?'

She refused to answer so he went and investigated for himself, lying out full length on her large divan bed and bouncing his hips a few times. 'Ah, that's better. Not much, but better.' He folded his arms behind his head and looked at Jane, who was glaring at him from the end of the bed. 'I don't suppose you'd like to swap?'

'No!'

He looked at her from under dark lashes. 'Or share?'

She jerked her eyes away from that hypnotic glitter.

'What's the matter, Jane? Does it disturb you to have me in your bed? Mmm...' He turned his head and rubbed his cheek against the pillow, sniffing, reminding her vividly of how erotic he had found the scent of their lovemaking.

'You can't stay here!' she said raggedly. 'I won't let you—'

'What are you going to do, call the police and have

me thrown out?' His eyes were bright blue with curiosity. 'Because that's the only way you're going to get rid of me.'

She was searching for a suitably devastating put-down when the phone rang. He groaned and got up to answer it. It was his secretary and he was immediately all business, sitting down at the desk, switching on his laptop and talking as he called up a series of files.

She went out into the kitchen, wishing she could slam things around to express her frustration but prevented by her injured hands. She had to be content with muttering to herself under her breath. By his confident behaviour he was implying that she had *expected* him to chase after her, whereas nothing was further from the truth. She wasn't going to take the blame for his predatory sexual instincts!

'Where's your vacuum cleaner?'

She jumped. 'What?'

'I thought I'd vacuum my room...bed included. Where do you keep the vacuum cleaner?'

'I don't,' she told him with malicious satisfaction. 'There's only an old-fashioned carpet sweeper.' He opened his mouth. 'And don't you *dare* have one delivered or I'll chuck it in the tide.'

'Like doing things the hard way just for the sake of it, do you, Jane?'

She looked as haughty as it was possible to do in a slightly grubby T-shirt and shorts. 'What's the matter, Ryan, too used to soft living to expend a bit of honest domestic elbow-grease? I don't think I'm going to need the police to get rid of you; the petty inconveniences of living down here will do it for me!'

He shrugged and turned away and she yelled after him with relish, 'Just remember you're supposed to be conserving water and electricity. And you can get your own meals, too. I'm not going to pay the price of your extravagance!'

A growl rolled back down the hall, and a short time later she heard the thumping rattle of the old carpet sweeper. She watched him haul his mattress out into the yard, as she had done with her own two weeks ago, and attack it with the side of a broom, releasing clouds of dust that frosted his dark hair and made her bite her lip to stop herself laughing. She stopped laughing when he efficiently remade his bed with fresh sheets he found for himself in a crammed linen closet and started poking about, investigating the building's structural deficiencies.

To avoid his disruptive presence Jane snatched up a towel and a book on self-sufficiency and went down to the beach, only to have Ryan settle down on the sand less than a metre away, wearing electric blue swimming briefs that left nothing to the imagination.

Without even asking her, he dug a faded beach umbrella—which she recognised as coming from a jumble of beach furniture in the garage—into the sand and angled it so that she was fully protected from the sun. Then he lay down on his towel and slowly massaged sunscreen over his thickly muscled body. If she had been wearing sunglasses Jane might have been able to safely ogle him in secret, but she had only the brim of Great-Aunt Gertrude's moth-eaten straw hat to hide behind, and consequently had to pretend not to notice his actions.

Since she couldn't go in the water, except to paddle, Jane hadn't bothered to struggle into a swimsuit, but now she felt a desperate need to cool off, especially when a passing bikini-clad blonde detoured from her path to laughingly offer to do Ryan's back.

He grinned as he modestly refused. 'My girlfriend is very jealous,' he said, casting a look at pink-faced Jane. 'She looks fairly innocuous, doesn't she? But, believe me, she's a tigress when she's defending her territory.'

She was still boiling at the memory later that evening, when Ryan refused to allow her into the kitchen to heat up some soup for her dinner, propping a chair under the doorhandle and ignoring her strident demands and savage kicks at the solid panels while he cooked up a storm. He finally let her in, but only when she had grudgingly agreed to share his meal.

The fact that his colourful stir-fry of vegetables and noodles was more delicious than anything Jane had yet cooked for herself added to her resentment. She was only slightly mollified by the sight of some of her bread, salvaged from the morning's accident, cut into neat triangles and generously buttered.

He had taken her at her word about the electricity and set candles on the kitchen table instead of using the overhead light, the warm, flickering glow creating a romantic atmosphere that Jane hadn't reckoned on when she had whined about the power bill. But for once Ryan was the perfect gentleman, allaying her fears as she ate by chatting about how he had learned to cook when his mother was doing shift work, how he had also looked after his baby sister, Melissa, and how his mother was now married to a chef who owned two restaurants, one of them in partnership with his stepson.

Jane said very little, concentrating on gingerly balancing her fork between the good fingers of her left hand, and as soon as dinner was over announced her intention of going to bed to read.

'Is that wise straight after eating?' frowned Ryan. 'Why don't we go for a stroll along the beach? The moon won't be over the hills yet, but I have a torch in the Rover.'

Warm night, dark beach, crashing waves, sexy man... Jane could feel her heart palpitating at the possibilities.

'I'm too tired,' she said truthfully. Too tired to feel like wrestling her own desires as well as his! Ryan's swift first aid had prevented her burn penetrating through many layers of her skin, but it was still smarting quite badly.

He followed her down the hall and watched her put the candle she was carrying on the low cabinet by her bed. 'How are you planning to wash? After a hot day like today I know you must be dying for a nice soap-down so your skin is soft and clean when you slide between the sheets, but now you've got *both* hands out of commission.'

His words were so evocative that Jane instantly felt every grain of sand and every microscopic speck of dust weighing like boulders on her sun-parched skin.

'My left one is much better than it was. I'll manage.'

'Not if your fork-handling is anything to go by. Don't be silly, Jane. You'll take ages and probably hurt yourself in the process. Why not let me give you a nice wash?'

Jane turned around, her mouth falling open. Standing in the doorway of her room, the devil even managed to look pious as he said, 'You'll feel much better afterwards.'

She could just imagine!

Her jaw snapped shut. 'I think I'll skip a wash tonight!'

He stepped over the threshold, seemingly undismayed by her vehement refusal. In the candlelit shadows he looked very big and very dark. 'What about your night-things? What do you wear to bed?'

With her injured hand she had found it easier to sleep nude than struggle into one of the silky confections that the valuers had fastidiously overlooked. 'None of your business.'

He took another step. 'I see,' he said and from the huskiness in his voice she saw all too well. 'But maybe with me in the house you'd feel more secure if you wore something. Do you need me to help you get undressed?'

She shook her head, biting her tongue. He came closer and fingered the bottom of her T-shirt. 'Are you sure?'

She nodded dumbly.

'What about your bra? Does it fasten at the front or back?'

'Back,' she whispered. Trust him to know that her bra was the weak point in her defence. She had tried going braless after she had broken her hand, but her size had made it uncomfortable and she had been too self-conscious about the way her breasts moved beneath her clothes to go out that way in public. Putting on a bra with only one good hand had been difficult, but not impossible, but now...

Jane closed her eyes, surrendering to the inevitable. But he didn't pull off her T-shirt. His hands were warm as they skimmed her waist under the loose fabric, separating to slide up around her ribs and meet again at the centre of her back. His breath was just as warm on her forehead as he deftly unhooked the tiny fastening and her full breasts shifted, settling lower on her chest, lightly brushing against his...

They stood for a frozen moment, then Jane felt him sigh and his hands fell away as he stepped back. She opened her eyes. His gaze was sombre, steady.

'If you want any more help, you'll have to ask for it.'

She couldn't say it. She just couldn't get the words out of her fear-locked throat, past her stubborn lips.

His nostrils flared and his features seemed to tighten, accentuating the broad, flat cheekbones and thrust of his jaw.

Without a word he peeled off her T-shirt and gently slid the bra down her arms. He knelt and unzipped her shorts and drew them off, along with her panties. Not once did he take his eyes off hers.

He rose to turn back her bed and guided her down onto the cool white cotton, draping the top sheet carefully over her voluptuous nudity. Then he left the room, returning a few minutes later with a bowl of warm soapy water, a face cloth, a towel and her hair brush.

Silently, rinsing the cloth often, he sat on the side of

the bed and slowly washed her face, throat and shoulders, and the upper swell of her breasts that rose above
the folded sheet. His face was a fascinating golden mask
in the candlelight as he patted her skin softly dry and
loosened her hair from its pony-tail, brushing it out in a
wavy black fan across the white pillow.

He leant over and blew out the candle, and in the
velvety blackness she felt his lips press briefly over her
ruffled brow, her eyes—each in turn—and her mouth.
Then, still without speaking, he was gone, closing the
door behind him with a quiet click.

CHAPTER EIGHT

HE WAS driving her crazy!

Four days later her uninvited house guest was still firmly ensconced, and Jane's peace and quiet had been irrevocably shattered. The phone was constantly ringing and Ryan was a perpetual whirlwind of activity. If he wasn't firing off memos and faxes or conducting conference calls, he was despatching his domestic duties with infuriating efficiency or tackling some of the most urgently needed repair work on the house with tools and materials he had salvaged from the garage.

He seemed impervious to the discomforts of the cramped cottage—indeed, seemed to treat the daily drudgery as a challenge! If she escaped down to the beach he imposed his presence on her there, too—jogging, body-surfing, leafing through reports or pestering her with conversation that was impossible to ignore. He was every bit as relentless on his mission of mercy as he had been at pursuing his vengeance.

'Don't you ever relax?' she had grumbled at him on the second evening, when he was once again nagging at her to play a game of chess rather than curling up next to the oil lamp with her book. For all he wouldn't let her lift a finger he seemed determined to involve her in everything he did.

He looked genuinely surprised. 'I *am* relaxed.'

'If this is you relaxed I'd hate to see you excited,' she said drily, and instantly regretted her words when his eyes gleamed with amusement.

'You already have,' he reminded her. 'And you didn't hate it at all.'

133

She scrunched deeper in the comfy old easy chair, wishing he didn't look so impossibly sexy in black. His trousers and short-sleeved shirt were plain, and unadorned by designer labels, yet somehow were rendered elegant by the wearer. He could ring the changes in a wardrobe that seemed to mysteriously grow larger by the day while Jane was forced by convenience to wear whatever was easiest to put on—usually the ubiquitous shorts and T-shirt.

She tossed her head. She didn't care how she looked, she was no longer one of the dress-to-impress brigade.

'I *meant* you seem to think you have to fill every waking moment with activity,' she said, watching him set out the chess pieces he had found in some dusty corner. 'The only time you rest is when you're sleeping.'

She'd used to be like that, too, she realised—constantly wound up, always restlessly looking for the next challenge, alert for the next stab in the back from friend or foe. Until it had all been snatched away from her she hadn't realised how subtly it had ground down her enjoyment of life.

He shrugged. 'It comes naturally to me. I've worked hard all my life. In fact, this is the closest thing I've had to a holiday for years.' His eyelids drooped as he remembered that the last holiday he had planned was going to be his honeymoon.

Jane shifted uncomfortably under his stare. 'Ava always said you found business more interesting than you did her,' she blurted, unknowingly echoing his thoughts.

He abandoned the chess pieces to come prowling across the room. 'Did she come running to you with all her petty complaints about my shortcomings?'

'They weren't petty, not to Ava.'

'Obviously not. But if she had come to me with them, instead of you, we might have worked them out.'

'I doubt it,' said Jane involuntarily, remembering Ava's soft brown eyes brimming with anguished tears

over her love for Conrad. Whatever Ryan had suffered,
at least he hadn't had to cope with the added humiliation
of knowing he was being dumped for a man who didn't
have a tenth of his personal charisma.

His eyes narrowed as they always did when he aimed
one of his stinging verbal darts. 'Didn't I satisfy her in
bed? Was that why she was so quick to believe I'd been
having an affair with someone else?'

'You weren't even sleeping together—' Jane protested, and bit her lip as she realised the trap he had set.

He looked grimly satisfied by her admission that she
had been privy to the most intimate details of his relationship with Ava. 'Did she also tell you why?'

'It was none of my business,' she said, looking away.
Maybe if she hadn't actively discouraged Ava's early
confidences about her relationship with Ryan events
might not have been forced to such a drastic turn. But
she had dealt with the fierce envy that she had felt whenever Ava had talked about Ryan by appearing to be supremely uninterested.

'I guess you knew she was still a virgin. She said she
wanted to wait until we were married,' he said softly,
his shrewd gaze on Jane's guiltily averted face. 'Did you
encourage her in that view, during your girlish chats, by
any chance...?'

Jane's blue eyes flashed as her chin tilted proudly up.
'Oh, no, you don't—you can't blame me for *that*! I never
did understand how she could—' She clamped her jaw
shut before she said too much.

'What? Deny me? Resist me?' he probed, with a trace
of his former silky malice. 'I know *you* find me sexually
irresistible, Jane,' he said, making her blush. 'But we're
talking about someone with a strong sense of morality
and an innate shyness.'

Jane couldn't help snorting. It hadn't been morality
that had stopped Ava from sleeping with her fiancé—it

had been her love for another man. She certainly hadn't been shy with Conrad!

'Whereas you...' he murmured speculatively. 'I think that if *you* were in love with a man, he wouldn't be able to keep you *out* of his bed.'

Her flush deepened as she thought of the wanton way she had behaved in that hotel room. 'If you're implying that I have no sense of morality...'

'Not at all. I'm just saying that once you commit yourself to a course of action you commit yourself utterly—no half measures, no holding back...full steam ahead and damn the torpedoes! A lot of people find that kind of overwhelming strength of purpose intimidating, especially in a woman.'

'That's *their* problem!' declared Jane, not sure whether to be flattered or insulted by his character sketch.

'I agree. Fortunately it's not mine. I'm not easily intimidated.' He rubbed his jaw reminiscently.

'Nor am I,' she said, staring resentfully up at his towering figure. 'So you can forget about hassling me into a chess game. *I'm* relaxing with a book, and when I've finished this chapter I'm going to go to bed—to sleep,' she added hurriedly.

He didn't move away. 'I'm not used to having such early nights. I'm having trouble sleeping. I toss and turn for hours in my lonely bed—'

'Probably the lumps in the mattress,' said Jane repressively, warned by the wicked quirk at the corner of his mouth.

'One lump in particular,' he agreed. 'Care to come to my room and help me smooth it out?'

With difficulty she kept her eyes on his, acutely aware that his hips were level with her face. 'Sorry—no hands,' she said sweetly, holding up her bandaged mitts.

'You won't need them; you can use your mouth—I happen to know you have a very versatile tongue,' he shot back silkily, and laughed at her glowering expression, sending a kick of exhilaration along her nerves. 'Walked right into that one, didn't you, sweetheart? You know, I think you're right—an idle chat is far more relaxing than a tense battle of chess that takes all one's concentration.'

He stretched his impressive musculature, abandoning the chessboard to stroll over to the couch where she was sitting with her book in her lap. 'Let's just sit here cosily together and talk some more about ourselves...'

That was the *last* thing she wanted, since he had an infuriating knack of provoking her into saying things that were better left unsaid.

So, of course, they had ended up playing chess, with Jane being roundly beaten even though all Ryan's concentration had definitely *not* been on the game.

The trouble was that no matter how absorbed he appeared to be in his own activities he always seemed to know where Jane was and what she was doing.

She couldn't even potter about in the garden without his interference. Only this morning she had waited until he was safely engaged in his morning conference call to his office before sneaking out to the garden to do some surreptitious weeding. She had only just worked out a painless technique, using a short length of bamboo stake to burrow under the weed roots and flick them out of the soil, when a shadow loomed and the stick was whipped from her hand.

'Do you have to do this right *now*?'

His irritation was music to her ears. 'Yes.'

He sighed heavily. 'Tell me what to do.'

'Don't tempt me,' she said sarcastically, eyeing the stick in his hand.

He looked down at her, kneeling at the edge of the garden. 'I know you're frustrated by the enforced inactivity, but I don't want you getting that dressing dirty now that those blisters are oozing.'

'You don't want me doing *anything*!' she burst out irritably. That soothing, reasonable voice of his got on her nerves. She didn't want him to be kind, she wanted him to be angry and hostile and easy to hate.

'Just following doctor's orders,' he said. 'Most women would be pleased at having a man run around at their beck and call.'

'Running around maybe, riding roughshod *over* no!'

'I'm just trying to help—'

'Are you? Or are you just here to enjoy watching me suffer?'

Her bitter utterance was followed by a pregnant silence. He crouched down beside her. 'I'm sorry if you believe that,' he said gravely. 'Maybe it was true—once. But that was before I got to know you—'

She bristled. 'You *don't* know me—'

'As well as anyone, I suspect. The fact that your best friend lives in Wellington says it all, really, doesn't it, Jane? You don't like people getting too close. You'd rather keep them at arm's length, in case they find out you aren't as tough as you pretend to be.'

She stiffened. Was that pity she heard in his voice? 'Spare me your cheap psychoanalysis.'

'Don't be so defensive. I'm trying hard to build up some trust here, Jane—how about meeting me halfway? We've both been guilty of malice and misjudgement in the past. You said you were searching for new beginnings at Piha. So why won't you begin by accepting my offer of friendship?'

'Because you don't want to be *friends*,' she said harshly.

'Lovers are friends, Jane.'

She flinched.

'Not always,' she denied. There had been nothing *friendly* about their sexual encounter in the hotel. And James—he had never mixed sex with friendship, either. As far as he had been concerned making love to Jane had been just a shrewd business move, an attempt to cement her loyalty.

'Have you had many?'

Her eyebrows shot up haughtily. 'Friends?'

'Lovers.'

'One or two.' She tried to sound blasé and to her chagrin he took her literally, thereby guessing the truth.

'Well, I didn't take your virginity so I guess that makes me number two,' he said teasingly. 'Was I better than the other guy?'

She jumped to her feet, gesturing towards the carrots with a shaking hand. 'Those need to be weeded and thinned out or their growth will be restricted,' she said, quoting the gardening guide she had consulted that morning.

'I take it that's a "yes"!' he called after her as she retreated hastily back into the house.

God, he was infuriating, she thought now, as she found a box of old clothes to sort through, most of all when he was right!

If only she could figure out his true motive for inflicting his presence on her. If it wasn't revenge, if he felt genuine remorse for reducing her to her present circumstances, surely he would have granted her her plea to be left alone?

And if he had come here to seduce her, why didn't he just get on with it with his usual relentless efficiency, dammit, instead of playing this drawn-out game of cat and mouse?

That first, bewildering night had set the scene. Ryan had the unique ability to tease her, annoy her, irritate her with his 'take charge' bossiness, only, in the next breath, to confuse her with such tender caring that she was in danger of believing in miracles... Then, just when he had her on the verge of surrender, aching for him to ruthlessly take advantage of her heightened vulnerabil-

ity, he would withdraw, leaving her hollow with loneliness and seething with physical frustration.

Also, he had a way of looking at her—just looking—
through half-closed eyes that reminded her of those
heated hours they had spent together in that hotel room
and the way he had looked at her then—all fury and
wild desire. And once the memory was roused it was
infuriatingly difficult to dislodge from her consciousness.

In this she was her own worst enemy. She should
never have allowed him to continue to perform those
intimate personal services—helping her dress and undress, brushing her hair each morning and night, dressing
her wound—but she had been unable to deny herself the
exquisite torture of his touch. She was an intelligent
woman; she could have found a way around her temporary disabilities if she had really tried. Instead, while
she had whined loudly at him for curtailing her freedom,
a wicked part of her, a primitive throwback to pre-
liberated times, had secretly wallowed in her helpless-
ness.

It had to stop!

The situation was more innocent yet potentially far
more dangerous than the one from which she had escaped. She could imagine the screaming headlines if the
Press found out that Jane Sherwood had the millionaire
tycoon who had caused her financial ruin acting as her
unpaid domestic slave. They would come up with all
sorts of kinky scenarios to explain the bizarre set-up—
and they wouldn't be far wrong—she thought with a
frisson of excitement at the memory of some of the de-
viant desires that Ryan aroused in her breast.

Oh, God, what if Ryan had *planned* for the story to
leak to the Press? He was quite capable of such
Machiavellian cunning. But no. She hastily dismissed
the idea. For it would be Ryan's reputation that would
suffer most if they were embroiled in a sex scandal that

implied he was some kind of S&M freak who enjoyed playing a submissive role.

She was still brooding on the alarming possibilities when there was a sharp knocking on the front door. Assuming the worst, she opened the door warily, but it was no sleazy journalist lurking on the sagging porch.

'Is Ryan in?'

Jane stared at the tall, skinny, sulky-looking redhead in the skin-tight acid-green dress who stood tapping a sandalled foot on the cracked boards, oozing hostile impatience. Parked haphazardly next to the four-wheel drive was a sporty convertible, its engine still ticking.

'Uh, yes.'

'Good.' Without waiting to be invited, the young woman brushed past Jane into the house, her green eyes darting curiously about, widening at the sight of peeling paintwork and faded furniture.

'Where is he—in here?' She headed towards the hum of the fax machine in the living room.

Jane felt her blood begin to simmer. How dared Ryan invite a strange woman to her home? Especially a beautiful, long-legged waif who made Jane feel like a clumping Amazon.

'No, he's out the back, digging in the garden,' she said sourly.

'The garden! But Ryan *hates* gardening!' The statement came out shrill and accusing.

Jane smiled into her incredulous face, enjoying a petty sense of revenge on both of them.

'I know. Isn't he a darling? He just can't seem to do enough for me!' she trilled, earning herself a vitriolic glare from kohl-lined eyes as her visitor rushed to find the back door. Her coltish grace made Jane realise that under the sophisticated make-up the waif was younger than she had first appeared—much too young for a hardened cynic like Ryan Blair.

Cradle-snatcher! she thought balefully as the girl ran

towards Ryan, the long red locks—which could only have come from a bottle—flouncing down her back as she called out his name.

She was only slightly mollified by the dismay on Ryan's face as he rose to his feet, a clutch of wispy carrot plants dripping from his large hand. So...he hadn't been expecting a visit from his little totty!

A moment later he dropped the carrots as the girl launched herself into his arms for a hug that made Jane's bones ache. They fitted together with the ease of long-standing intimacy. Jane folded her arms across the tightness in her chest as the pair began an animated conversation, the girl's thin arms gesticulating wildly and Ryan's body language surprisingly defensive. Good! She hoped he was having a great deal of trouble explaining himself!

He saw Jane still standing on the verandah and slung his arm across the girl's narrow shoulders, tugging her back towards the house in spite of her obvious reluctance.

'I hope Melissa wasn't rude. Sometimes she tends to act first and think later when family matters are at stake,' he said, coming up the steps.

'*Melissa?*' Jane echoed faintly as the truth hit her. She tried not to gape as she compared the sulky, slinky creature in front of her to the vague memory of a plump brown-haired sixteen-year-old trailing Ava down the aisle. No wonder the hostile green eyes had seemed so familiar. Although she had never met Ryan's sister she recalled Ava describing how excited Melissa had been about being a bridesmaid for the first time and how much she had loved her frothy dress.

Ryan was digesting her ill-concealed shock. 'Of course...who did you think she was?' he asked curiously.

Jane stiffened. 'I had no idea, since she didn't stop to introduce herself,' she said coldly, to hide her chagrin.

She was so busy grappling with the implications of Melissa's arrival that she allowed herself to be hustled into the kitchen where Ryan calmly set about the ritual of morning tea.

'Jealous, Jane?' he murmured in her ear as he moved past her to place the kettle on the stove.

'In your dreams!' she muttered, haughtily ignoring his knowing smile, aware of Melissa's resentful regard.

'Oh, yes—frequently...' His soft words were accompanied by a brief resting of his hand on her hip, ostensibly to move her out of the way so he could reach the mugs on the shelf behind her.

'You still haven't been formally introduced, have you?' he said as they all sat down at the kitchen table. 'Jane Sherwood, my sister Melissa, who's an aspiring model—'

Melissa's head jerked back. 'I'm not *aspiring*. I already *am* a model!'

'Part-time—'

'Only until my career takes off. As soon as I get more jobs than I can fit in with my lectures I'm dropping out. I can always go back to university later—'

It was obviously an old argument. 'But you won't. It's much harder to get back into studying after years away from it. I don't know why you can't continue to fit your modelling around your lectures.'

'Because a modelling career doesn't last very long—'

'So much more reason to have other qualifications to fall back on.'

'So you have to strike while the iron's hot, make the most of your opportunities when they occur. If I want to succeed I have to make myself available when photographers want me to be available, not the other way around.'

'What do you think?' Ryan asked Jane unexpectedly.

'What's it got to do with *her*?' snarled Melissa, tossing her head in a swirl of fire.

'Absolutely nothing,' said Jane flatly. 'It's your life. What you do with it is entirely up to you.' She looked across at Ryan. 'Don't let *anybody* tell you any different.'

She could see that Melissa was torn between the desire to use the comment to support her own views and the equally strong desire not to agree with anything Jane said.

'Troublemaker!' said Ryan. 'Here—' he dunked a straw into Jane's mug. 'Drink your tea. Jane wanted to be a dress designer but she let her father bully her into business,' he told his sister.

Again that flicker of confusion as Melissa frowned at the dressing and tape on Jane's hands. 'I don't see why I should be expected to feel sorry for *her*,' she burst out, gnawing on her pouting red lips. 'Or why *you* had to move in with her. I couldn't *believe* it when I found out where you were—'

'I've already explained all that.'

So that's what they had been discussing so heatedly in the garden. Jane would have traded her last cent to have heard his explanation!

'But—'

'Melissa!'

The quiet thunder only slightly subdued the girl's rebelliousness. 'I only wanted to ask why it had to be *here*!' She cast a disparaging look around the kitchen, much as her brother had done several days before. 'At least up the hill you'd have tons more room and all the mod cons!'

'Up the hill?' Jane frowned in puzzlement.

The breath hissed through Ryan's teeth as Melissa said sullenly, 'At our place. Why couldn't you have stayed there instead of making my brother live in this dump?'

'I didn't *make* him do anything,' gritted Jane, before the true import of Melissa's words sank in. No wonder

Ryan had wanted to shut his sister up! 'Wait a minute...*your* place? Are you saying that you have a bach here at Piha?'

Melissa laughed scornfully. 'I'd hardly call a five-bedroomed house on three acres of headland bush a "bach"!' It was her turn to frown as she looked from Jane's blank shock to her brother's annoyed expression. 'You didn't know? You didn't *tell* her we had a house here?' she asked Ryan in a deeply disconcerted tone of voice.

'No, he didn't tell me!' said Jane, feeling just as unhappy as she glared at the culprit.

He had the gall to shrug coolly. 'Since you were adamant you wouldn't leave here, it didn't seem relevant. Besides, technically the house isn't mine—I bought it for our family trust a couple of years ago.'

'Not *relevant*!' she repeated with outraged shrillness.

'Well, was it? Would you have accepted an invitation to be my guest while your hand healed?'

'No! But I didn't invite you to stay here, either, and that didn't stop you going ahead and doing it anyway!' she pointed out.

'Because you're too stubborn to admit you need help with everything but the lightest of tasks. I'm not leaving you alone until you can prove otherwise—'

'Why don't you just hire a nurse for her?' Melissa interrupted truculently.

'Because Jane is my *personal* responsibility,' said Ryan, with a faint emphasis that made Jane flush. 'And as you know, Mel, I always take my responsibilities seriously.'

The quiet implacability of his statement sounded like a warning, although Jane wasn't sure whether it was intended for herself or his sister. But Melissa obviously possessed a full measure of the dogged Blair tenacity, for while she appeared to let the subject drop she returned to it from different angles again and again, with terrier-like persistence.

'But it's mid-term break—you know I only have a week off. If you're going to be down here you should at least be staying with *us*.'

Jane could have retreated to her room, but she was not going to be driven even further into exile by this family. If they wanted to discuss their private business then *they* would be the ones to withdraw. So she sat in silence, her face a mask of haughty indifference as she sipped her tea, secretly fascinated by the interaction between brother and sister.

Ryan was revealing another facet of himself, mild and restrained, as he dealt with Melissa's youthful dramatics. The deep bond of their affection for each other was revealed in the freedom with which they argued, unconstrained by fear of being rejected or belittled for their beliefs. Even though they sparred vigorously there was none of the bitterness that had characterised Jane's father's attacks on her actions and opinions.

It was something Jane had never had, and envied horribly—that easy affection, that wonderful security of knowing that you're loved whatever you say or do. So she was almost sympathetic when Ryan briefly left the room to check an incoming fax and Melissa rounded on her like a virago.

'As far as I'm concerned you deserve everything that's happened to you! If you think you can sink your claws into my brother you've got another think coming!'

'I don't think there's much danger of my doing that at the moment,' said Jane wryly, indicating her damaged hands.

'I don't believe that pathetic helpless act for one minute.' The green eyes blazed fiercely. 'And I bet Ryan doesn't, either! He said you were a lying, scheming bitch!'

'Then you have nothing to worry about, do you?'

Ryan came back before Melissa could think of a comeback but, a few minutes later, she jumped up from the table.

'Well, if you're not going to stay up at the house, then neither am I,' she announced dramatically to her brother. 'I'm going to stay here with you!'

While Jane gaped at her presumption, Ryan merely leaned against the sink, looking indulgently amused. '*You*—in *this* dump? Where there's no running hot water, no television and you have to do your laundry by hand?'

Melissa looked briefly aghast before tossing her head in annoyance. 'If you can hack it, so can I. I'm driving up to get my things. I'll be back as soon as I can.'

And with a triumphant look at Jane's stunned face she flounced out of the house.

Jane recovered her voice. 'She's not serious, is she?' she cried, crossing to the window to watch the girl fling herself behind the wheel of her jazzy yellow car and rev it unnecessarily as she backed into a turn. 'Does she think I'm running a free boarding house for stray Blairs? It's ridiculous! One uninvited guest is bad enough. If she comes back you tell her she can't possibly stay here!'

Ryan shrugged as he put their cups in the sink. 'Once Mel gets an idea into her head it's difficult to dislodge it. She's very big on family togetherness. For a long time I was the father figure in her life, and even after Mum married Steve I was the one to whom Mel looked for primary advice and guidance—consequently she's rather possessive of me.'

He gave Jane a sly, sidelong look. 'As soon as she found out I was here with you she came hotfoot to check the situation for herself. For some reason she seems to think I need protecting from your wicked wiles.'

'Maybe the reason being that you told her I was a lying, scheming bitch,' said Jane acidly.

'Ah, well…' He spread his hands ruefully. 'Perhaps she did overhear me say a few uncomplimentary things about you in the past.'

'How did she find out where I was? How many other people know you're here?' she asked jerkily, feeling the world she had escaped threatening to close in on her again.

'Just Carl, Irene—my secretary—Graham Frey…and my mother, of course. As far as everyone else is concerned I'm having a break from deadly office routine at the family holiday home—'

But Jane's brain had frozen. 'Your *mother*?'

He looked at her gravely. 'There are no secrets in my family, Jane. We've always been frank with each other. Mothers tend to worry if they don't know where their children are, even when they're adults.'

Oh, God… 'What did you tell them? How much does Melissa know about me?'

'Everything.'

'*Everything?*' Jane was appalled; her hands rose to her hot cheeks.

Gently Ryan shackled her wrists and pulled her arms down, preventing her from hiding her devastated expression. 'I don't mean the intimate details—that I tried to treat you like a prostitute and you tried to treat me like a one-night stand. I don't involve my sister in my sex life,' he said, ruthlessly excising her shame. 'But she certainly knows the rest—what your father did to ours was always openly discussed in our house, and she knew I was obsessed with getting revenge on him, and then on you…'

She couldn't look at him. 'So she knows that it was me—at the wedding—'

'Of course. My family believed in me, even if others were quick to condemn—they deserved to know their faith was justified. They didn't agree with my decision to protect Ava by refusing to make a scandal out of your lies, but because they loved me they accepted it and supported me with their silence—even though it strained some of their own friendships.'

'Oh, God...' She shivered. No wonder Melissa had looked at her with hatred and contempt.

Ryan's hands ran up and down the back of her goose-pimpled arms, warming the chill from her skin, pulling her against the solid column of his body. Their height difference was accentuated by her lack of shoes, and Jane's nipples tightened treacherously against the lace of her bra as her belly nudged his denim-clad hips.

'You were cold then, too... Your voice had that emotional frigidity you assume whenever you're most frightened,' he murmured against her forehead. 'You were so damnably convincing in your humiliated dignity that for one nightmarish moment I nearly believed it myself. Why won't you talk about it with me? Is it anything to do with Ava—why she was so quick to forgive you? Help me to understand.'

She had stiffened within the circle of his arms at his shattering admission, now she pushed at his chest with panicky elbows.

Ava! His voice always softened on her name. Perhaps speaking to her on the telephone had reawakened some of his old feelings, and if he was still carrying a torch for her then to discover how thoroughly she had betrayed his love and trust would be even more deeply humiliating now than a quick, cruel dose of the bitter truth would have been three years ago. Who wanted to be told they had spent years cherishing a shining memory that was in reality a pitiful lie? He might feel justified in lashing out with another destructive orgy of vengeance.

Either way, Jane would once again be caught in the middle. She had already revealed too much about herself to him over the last few days—being misunderstood was the last line of defence for her wary heart! 'I thought you'd already decided that it was the jealous spite of an old maid.'

There was wry humour in his voice as he let her go and tilted her chin with his fist. 'You may be old now but you were only twenty-three at the time. Oh, I can still accept the jealousy part, but not the spite. You're a fighter, but unlike your father—and me—you haven't proved to be very good at nursing a grudge. By all rights you should hate me with a passion, but instead, well...' He trailed off, his eyes moving down over the full breasts pushing against the soft T-shirt...down to delicately tanned legs revealed by her linen shorts.

'I do hate you,' she said quickly. Too quickly. His eyes gleamed and he dropped a kiss on her mouth, the kind of casual salute he had perfected purely to drive her mad.

'One day you're going to trust me enough to tell me what I want to know...'

And then he would walk away. 'Is that what all this pretence of caring is about? Persuading me to talk about the good old days?' she managed sarcastically.

He didn't even bother to argue that it wasn't a pretence. He merely gave her the bold, confident smile of a seasoned hunter. 'That...and seducing you back into my bed!'

Maybe there might be an advantage to having a hostile nineteen-year-old chaperon hanging around after all! Jane thought feverishly.

She was wrong.

Melissa arrived back as threatened, her small boot stuffed with a clutch of bags that necessitated Ryan shifting boxes from the third bedroom into the garage. She lavished her brother with laughing attention and hissed baleful insults at Jane whenever the two women were alone. She complained about anything and everything, especially the fact that Jane was being waited on hand and foot while she, Melissa, had to take on her share of the chores. At lunch she changed into another outfit designed to make Jane feel like a slattern for arriving at the table in the same T-shirt and shorts, and entertained Ryan with non-stop stories about people that Jane didn't know and cared less about.

In the afternoon she got a measure of her own back by going for a brisk walk along one of the bush tracks that linked up with other walking trails through the western Waitakeres. But her usual enjoyment of the hushed beauty of the native forest was compromised by the sound of Melissa panting and whining in her wake, constantly begging Ryan to slow down, or rest, or help her get the stones out of her sneakers, or identify some piece of flora or fauna—anything to prise him away from Jane's side.

Later, while Ryan was working at his computer and Jane was lying on an old rug in the garden sketching on some scrap paper, with a small pencil-stub lightly suspended between her left forefinger and thumb, she was joined by Melissa, who wore a minuscule string bikini that would have created a riot on the beach. Braced for another round of hostilities, Jane instead found herself listening to chapter and verse about the many, many beautiful, witty and wonderful women who charmed Ryan's existence, how marvellous a son and brother he was and how he would never do anything that would hurt his mother, especially after the hardships and disappointments she had suffered in the past...

A sledgehammer would have been more subtle.

Jane gritted her teeth through a chatter-filled dinner that Melissa had merrily helped her brother prepare and could barely raise a smile when Ryan firmly stated that she was making him nervous by hovering over his shoulder as he changed the dressing on Jane's burnt palm. He suggested she pour the pan of hot water on the stove into the sink to start the washing-up, and she immediately began complaining about the unnecessary strictures on the use of electricity.

'The little sister from hell,' Ryan murmured ruefully, gently peeling off the old dressing while Melissa clattered the plates indignantly into the sink behind them.

'You should know—you both come from the same origins,' Jane whispered tartly as they studied the shiny pink patches of new skin emerging from beneath the weeping blisters, but the hint of conspiracy in his amusement was irresistible. 'One minute she's the wicked witch of the Waitakeres, the next it's Pollyanna on speed,' she muttered. 'Is she ever going to run down?'

He chuckled. 'She's jealous.'

His soft reply feathered along her exposed nerves. 'I don't know why—I'm not making any claim on you...'

His eyes were very blue. 'A claim doesn't have to be verbal to exist. If she hasn't already guessed we're lovers she soon will...'

His whisper seemed as loud as a shout in her ears, and Jane flushed as she glanced guiltily at Melissa's expressively outraged back.

'*Ex*-lovers,' she said through her teeth. Her eyes fluttered down and she experimentally flexed her fingers and winced.

'Still painful?'

Jane nodded, grateful for the prosaic turn of the conversation. 'But only when I clench or stretch it...the rest of the time it's just uncomfortably tight.'

'Graham says to give it another few days under a light dressing, then you can leave it open to the air...' Much to Jane's embarrassment he was reporting her progress to his friend over the telephone each day, as if her moderate burn were of life-threatening importance.

After he had redressed the wound Jane left brother and sister finishing the dishes and sat in the lumpy old easy chair under the window in the lounge with her pencil and the sheaf of sketches that were beginning to germinate an idea in the back of her mind. When the others joined her she was sufficiently immersed to have the excuse of turning down Ryan's suggestion of a card game, so a two-handed game was played until Melissa tired of losing and perversely chose to take a dig at Jane's self-absorption by plucking up one of the sketches as it slipped off the faded arm of the chair.

The disdain slid off her mobile face, her eyes brightening with interest as she snatched up another drawing. 'Hey, fashion designs! Far out! I thought you were sketching boring scenery or something. I like this layered look—'

She suddenly remembered she was enthusing to the enemy and tried to affect uninterest as Jane explained that she had often sketched an outfit that she wanted her dressmaker to sew rather than choosing an existing design from a book of patterns or a fashion magazine.

It was left to Ryan to pick up the conversation and ask to see more of the painstakingly executed drawings, and his sister scowled when he expressed a surprised admiration that warmed Jane with pride. Melissa immediately trashed the moment by gushing about the designer who had made such a wonderful job of Ava's wedding and bridesmaids' dresses.

'I don't suppose Ava could bear to keep it after what happened...'

Ryan didn't turn a hair at this gross insensitivity. 'Perhaps she wore it for her second wedding and imbued it with happier memories,' he said sardonically.

Jane knew the pain he must be shielding with his cynicism. 'No, she and Conrad were married quietly in a register office—' She broke off, biting her lip as Ryan's gaze snapped to attention.

'Oh? Were you there?' Jane looked away. 'Were you one of their witnesses, Jane?'

'Yes,' she admitted uncomfortably.

'And a godmother to their first child, so I understand.

Curiouser and curiouser...' he said softly. He might have pursued his line of thought, but Melissa distracted him by deciding it was dark enough to turn on the lights and starting an argument when she discovered she was supposed to use lamps and candles that were probably a fire hazard or would give off toxic fumes, or burn up all the oxygen in the room.

By the following afternoon Jane was on the point of throttling her additional unwanted guest. There was no eluding Melissa's constant, carping, competitive chaperonage, and with Ryan refusing to budge or temper his possessive attitude towards Jane—indeed it had become subtly more intense since his sister's arrival—she was driven to deliver a gunfighter's ultimatum: the cramped cottage wasn't big enough for the three of them. The portable stereo with its head-banging music and floor-pounding bass had been the last straw.

As she'd expected, Ryan declined to tremble at the empty threat, but he did suggest a compromise—the only one he was prepared to consider.

If Jane agreed to spend the next few days in the five-bedroomed house up the hill then, as soon as her burnt hand was fully functional again, she could return to her cottage with a guarantee that she would be left in peace. In the meantime she would have all the privacy she desired, a superb cook/housekeeper to wait on her instead of Ryan's unsettling personal attentions, and Melissa kept firmly off her back.

'Is that possible?' said Jane wryly.

'In my house, she obeys my rules. If she doesn't like them, she can go back to Auckland.'

'And afterwards, when I come back here...you'll go away and leave me alone?' she said cautiously. 'That's a promise?'

His thick black eyelashes screened his eyes, his blunt, handsome features tight and inscrutable; his was a gambler's face, intent on winning the pot by out-reading the opposition.

'Yes, if that's what you want...'

CHAPTER NINE

NO WONDER Melissa had been so bitchy about the deprivations that her brother had been made to suffer, thought Jane several hours later as she left her room to wander through the magnificent two-storeyed holiday house perched on the headland above Piha. Compared to Great-Aunt Gertrude's, this place was a palace!

The long modern Mediterranean-style house was bounded at the rear by a dense stand of virgin native bush and the north-facing aspect captured the sun all day. The outflung arms of the building curved in a broad U-shape towards the cliff, as if reaching out to embrace the spectacular view, and from her upstairs bedroom, which opened out, like all the other bedrooms, onto its own private balcony, Jane could see the whole of Piha—even a wedge of the rusty iron roof that she had been persuaded to temporarily abandon.

Once he had had her agreement, the shift in premises had been accomplished with Ryan's usual ruthless efficiency, leaving little time for second thoughts. Jane had no reason to feel piqued that he had merely given her a brief tour of his house before disappearing with a vague murmur about letting her settle in. Melissa, too, had floated off, gleefully smug that her obnoxious behaviour had achieved one of her primary aims.

Jane had her doubts. She got the feeling that it was Ryan who had been the main orchestrater of events. Melissa had merely been the *deus ex machina* by which he had distracted and manoeuvred Jane into accepting a deal that she would otherwise have flatly refused to even consider. Ryan could hardly have continued to escalate his campaign of seduction in the poky little cottage, with his sister breathing down their necks, alert to every creak of the floorboards, every stray touch and heated look. But here, in comfort and luxury, with privacy locks on all the bedroom doors and little distraction from her rapidly healing burn, Jane was all too vulnerable to his dangerously seductive persistence.

Jane's mouth dried at the memory of Ryan's lovemaking and, since she had drifted in the general direction of the kitchen, she decided on a cold drink to cure her hot flush.

She hesitated at the door when she saw a small, spare, middle-aged woman with a short helmet of silver hair bustling back and forth between the sink and central work-island, obviously preparing vegetables for dinner. This must be the housekeeper who was employed on a part-time basis whenever the family was in residence, Jane guessed. The one that Ryan had mentioned was a superb cook.

She cleared her throat and the woman looked up from her chopping board, surprise springing into her warm hazel eyes at the sight of Jane in her plain skirt and white cotton T-shirt, her feet in classy black flats and her hair rioting loose around her bare face.

'Hello, I'm Jane Sherwood...' She faltered, not quite sure how to politely describe her turbulent relationship with Ryan.

'Yes, I know.' The woman's face lit up in a generous smile that made Jane feel like an old and valued friend. 'What an awful time you've been having, my dear. I'm Peggy Mason. I won't offer to shake hands because I know you can't. Come on in and sit down. You look hot...would you like an iced tea?' She put down her knife, drying her hands on her apron. 'I find it just the thing in this heat. Sit here and I'll get you one.'

She steered Jane onto a stool at the breakfast bar which divided the kitchen from an open living area, clicking her tongue sympathetically as she looked at the damaged hands. 'You poor thing—no wonder Ryan insisted you needed looking after. I bet it's terribly frustrating...like being a baby all over again. Now, would you like something to eat with your glass of tea? I know you had lunch before you came, but dinner won't be served until quite late...the family likes to eat out on the terrace and watch the sunset—'

'Uh, no thank you, Mrs Mason,' said Jane, disconcerted by her familiarity yet irresistibly drawn by the woman's maternal warmth.

'Call me Peggy.' She set down the iced tea and returned to her chopping, making little piles of celery and onion as she continued with a chiding frown, 'I hope you're not dieting. It's not a good thing to do when your body's been under a lot of pain or stress.'

'I have lost a bit too much weight recently,' Jane was amazed to hear herself confess. 'But not on purpose...and I think I'm starting to put it back on,' she added hurriedly as Peggy frowned and she sensed an impending scold.

But the housekeeper's vehement disapproval was directed elsewhere. 'Ryan has a lot to answer for! Melissa told me how you burnt your hand. I hope he apologised for causing you to hurt yourself!'

Jane's smile was rueful. 'Well, it was mostly my own stupidity...' Both times, she added mentally, flattening out the strapped fingers of her left hand and experiencing the faint twinge that reminded her that if she had obeyed her original orders the healing would have been complete by now.

Grey eyebrows rose sharply over hazel eyes. 'You're far too forgiving, my dear. A hefty dose of guilt is just what that boy needs to curb his tendency to play God!'

'Well, he appears to be trying to make up for it...' Jane said weakly, suddenly realising that Peggy wasn't just referring to her current physical injuries. By her easy manner she was obviously used to being treated as part of the family by the Blairs and must be aware of Ryan's vendetta, if not the reason for it. Her affection for him was plainly strong, but her natural sympathies seemed to lie with the underdog.

'Oh? In what way?'

Jane pinkened at the innocent question. 'Well, he's cooked me some marvellous meals,' she said hastily, burying her nose in her tea.

'Mmm...' Peggy gave her an assessing look. 'He's pretty handy in the kitchen, I'll give him that.'

And the bedroom! Jane's flush deepened as the thought popped into her head.

'I wish *I* was—a good cook, I mean,' she stammered. 'My technique is still very much trial and error. Unfortunately I never learned the basics when I was young...'

'Didn't your mother ever let you help her around the kitchen when you were little?'

'We always had a cook and I wasn't supposed to get in the way. My mother left home when I was six,' Jane added impulsively.

'I'm sorry,' said Peggy, with a quiet compassion that tapped a deep-seated need in Jane's subconscious.

'Actually, I don't remember that much about her, except that she was dark and pretty and liked to laugh and went out a lot,' she admitted, her eyes darkening with memory. 'After she left, my father burnt all her photos and only mentioned her when he was in a rage, so I'm not sure if what I remember is real or a childish fantasy I've built up in my head.'

'Do you mean you never saw her again after your parents separated?'

Jane looked down at the glass she was slowly turning around in her clumsy grip, missing the warning glance that the hazel eyes directed over her head.

'No...she was just there one day and gone the next. It wasn't until a week later that my father told me she'd run off to Canada with her lover. He said she'd told him she didn't want to be saddled with the responsibility of a whining little brat like me.'

Peggy almost dropped her knife, clearly appalled. 'He said *that* to a six-year-old child!'

Jane had never found it easy to confide in people, instilled with her father's belief that if you were strong you didn't bother other people with your problems, especially if they were emotional ones. But Peggy's empathy made it seem natural to open up.

'He used to say that the reason she never bothered to send me birthday cards was because she obviously preferred to forget I'd ever been born. He always managed to make me feel a failure for not being able to make her love me enough to stay...'

'That was very, *very* wrong of him,' Peggy said fiercely. 'It's *never* a child's fault when a marriage fails.'

'He wasn't just wrong—he was *lying*,' Jane blurted out. 'He lied about their being divorced and he lied about her not caring what happened to me. You see, after my father died I was going through his safety deposit box and I found some old letters and documents about their separation agreement and a wrangle over child access.

'My mother *had* gone to Canada with another man but she'd been killed in a car accident in Montreal a couple of months after she got there. Maybe she *hadn't* wanted to take me away with her, but it wasn't true that she wanted to pretend I never existed. There was correspondence from her lawyer, demanding assurances that I would be given any letters that she sent, and she'd asked my father to get me a passport so I could visit her. But then she was killed.

'She died—and for *years*, until I stopped letting him know how much I cared, my father told me she was having too much fun with her new life to send me a *birthday card*!'

There was a faint sound behind her and Jane jerked

around, almost spilling the rest of her tea. Ryan was standing in the doorway, and from the grim look on his face he had been there for quite some time.

'No wonder you believed me so easily when I told you about what your father had done to mine,' he rasped, entering the sunlit room, his white trousers and yellow shirt adding an extra dimension to its brightness. 'You knew it was just the kind of callous, conscienceless thing a bastard like him would do!'

'Ryan!' Peggy Mason's hazel eyes were full of reproach.

'Sorry, but it's the truth and we all know it.' Ryan sighed as he went over and kissed the finely lined cheek. 'Hello, Mum, what are you doing here...besides the obvious?' he said, looking wryly at Jane.

'You're Ryan's *mother*?' Jane experienced a sinking feeling in her stomach as she looked from the tiny woman with whom she had felt such an instant kinship to the giant towering beside her, searching in vain for a resemblance. Now she knew why the housekeeper had seemed so well informed!

'I thought you realised who I was when I introduced myself,' said Peggy in surprise. 'I'm sorry—I just assumed you'd know my second husband's surname. Who did you think I was?'

'Probably another of my girlfriends,' said Ryan cruelly. 'When Melissa turned up Jane thought she was some infatuated nymphet I was keeping on a string.'

'No, I didn't!' she snapped. She smiled apologetically at his mother, deciding that in the long run her ignorance had probably done her a favour, easing what could otherwise have been a hideously awkward meeting. 'I'm afraid I just assumed you were the housekeeper...'

Peggy's surprise turned to amused understanding. 'I see. And now you're embarrassed by your frankness. Don't be—I appreciated the insight and I'm sure you feel better for talking about it.'

'You still haven't told me why you're here, Mum,' interrupted Ryan. 'I thought you said Steve had some wedding parties booked for this week and would be too busy for you to come down. And why are you cooking instead of Teresa?'

'The school called for her to pick up her son—he apparently has chicken pox—so I told her that of course we could manage without a housekeeper for the next few days. And it's *because* Steve is going to be so busy that I thought I might as well come down and enjoy some of this wonderful beach weather.'

Ryan picked up a piece of celery and crunched it between strong white teeth as he studied her innocent expression. 'So you're saying that Melissa didn't phone you to tell you what we were doing? This surprise visit has nothing whatsoever to do with the fact that Jane and I are here—'

'Well, that is a bit of a bonus, darling.' His mother patted his hard cheek fondly. 'Since it's too rare these days that I get to enjoy the company of *both* my children on holiday at the same time. Ryan hardly ever spends time at Piha any more,' she said to Jane, who was beginning to realise that his mother was more than a match for Ryan's shrewdness. 'The last time I tried to get him to stay more than a weekend he was chafing at the bit by the second day.'

'I know what you mean,' Jane murmured wryly.

'Do you?' She tilted her head in bird-like enquiry. 'Has he been an awful nuisance?'

'No, I haven't! I've been trying to get Jane to rest. How long are you going to stay?' he asked bluntly.

'Well, I don't know...a few days at least—it depends on how I'm feeling. You know I don't usually have a timetable about these things.' The hazel eyes smiled at her son's open frustration.

'Steve'll miss you—'

'We don't live totally in each other's pockets, Ryan. It's not as if he's very far away.'

He muttered something under his breath.

'What did you say, darling?'

'Nothing,' he gritted.

Jane stood up, feeling awful. 'Oh, please! I think I should leave. I know you can't possibly want me in your home,' she said to the older woman. 'It's not as if I don't have somewhere to go—'

'No, dammit!'

'Nonsense, of course you mustn't leave.' Peggy's mellow voice of reason overrode Ryan's raw explosion. 'I've never believed in children being responsible for the sins of their fathers.' This was accompanied by a stern look that, to Jane's fascination, made Ryan thrust his bunched hands in his trouser pockets, his face darkening except for a thin white line around his compressed mouth.

'From the sound of it you were as much a victim of your father as I was, so let there be no awkwardness about the past. As for what happened with Ava, well…that's all water under the bridge now. Isn't that right, Ryan?'

He jerked his head, his eyes smouldering on Jane's embarrassed face. 'I've already told her that, but she won't believe me.'

His mother's mouth pursed. 'You do surprise me, Ryan, and after all you've done for her, too!'

He set his teeth at her sarcasm. 'I said I'd look after her and I will.'

'How magnanimous of you. I hope you don't expect her to feel grateful.'

Ryan wrenched a hand out of his pocket and ran it through his hair. 'For God's sake, Mum, what are you trying to do to me?'

His mother smiled serenely. 'Just checking, darling.'

Thinking that mother and son might like to have a

discussion in private, Jane asked if she could put some personal laundry into the washing machine. Peggy explained where it was, saying that if she needed help in doing anything she only had to ask for it.

She did her small load of washing and spent what remained of the afternoon and on into the evening leafing through the kind of fashion magazines she could no longer afford to buy, talking with Peggy in the kitchen and watching Melissa try to come to terms with her mother's kindness towards the enemy.

Whenever Ryan appeared his mother gave him a task to perform that involved them all, and at dinner he found himself at the opposite end of the table to Jane. Melissa cheered up at this evidence that her mother's kindness might be of the killing kind, and after dinner decided it was safe to drive down the road to party with a group of friends.

After she and Ryan had done the dishes, Peggy suggested a film that was showing on television—another luxury that Jane could no longer take for granted—and the three of them settled down to watch, Ryan exiled to a chair while the two women shared the couch. The film was a thriller with a strong thread of romance, and whenever there was a love scene Jane had to force herself to keep her eyes on the screen, conscious of the brooding looks Ryan was sending her way. As soon as the credits rolled he sprang to his feet and declared that Jane was looking tired and that he would see her to her room.

He had tugged her out of her comfortable seat and hustled her as far as the door when the arrival of an international call thwarted his intentions, and he scowled impotently as Peggy blandly offered to escort their guest upstairs while he took the call—since, if Jane was so *tired*, she wouldn't want to wait around heaven knew how long for Ryan to finish his business...

'I'm sorry for putting you to all this extra work while your housekeeper's away,' said Jane awkwardly, after her hostess had tactfully helped her to change into the baggy T-shirt she had taken to sleeping in. The older woman then produced some large rubber kitchen gloves so that Jane could wash her own face, an idea which, to her chagrin, had never occurred to her—not that Great-Aunt Gertrude appeared to have possessed any gloves—or to Ryan, who was supposed to be so clever! But, of course, it had been in his interests to encourage her continuing dependence on him!

'I'm enjoying it,' admitted Peggy, watching Jane sit down at the dressing table and begin gingerly brushing her hair. 'It's about time Ryan came to his senses. I warned him that he would regret it if he let his desire for revenge get out of hand, but of course he claimed that that would never happen. Now I think he's finally realised that two wrongs don't make a right!'

'That's not what Melissa thinks—' Jane winced as the bristles caught on a knot and the handle of the brush yanked free of the gentle grip of her left hand.

'Here, let me do that,' said Peggy, picking up the brush and taking over where Jane had left off. 'Melissa still sees everything in black and white. She doesn't see that there might be wider issues at stake or extenuating circumstances. To her, there are no shades of grey.'

'And I'm a *very* grey area,' said Jane wryly.

'Oh, a veritable grey hole.' Peggy's eyes twinkled in the mirror.

Jane swallowed. She had to say it. 'I don't know why you're being so nice to me. I mean, after what I did to Ryan...those awful lies I told to break up the wedding...the scandal...you must have hated me...'

Peggy put down the brush and sighed. 'Hate is such a self-destructive emotion. I was shocked, certainly, but to tell you the truth when Ava returned Ryan's ring I wondered if it wasn't all for the best.'

'But Melissa told me you were heartbroken that Ryan didn't marry Ava.'

The older woman sat on the bed. 'Melissa exaggerates. What I wanted—what I still want—is for Ryan to be happy. I don't know how much he's told you about himself, but revenge was the driving obsession of his life for over a decade. The need to make your father pay for what he did shaped his ambitions and absorbed all of his emotional energy.

'When he found out that your father was dying and forced himself to relinquish his obsession I was very proud of him—no revenge is more honourable than the one not taken. But it meant that suddenly there was a huge emotional void in his life, and I think he instinctively sought to fill it with the utter antithesis of the ugliness, the greed and corruption that had obsessed him for so long...someone soft and quiet and gentle whom he could cherish and protect and never have any desire to hurt.

'He has very highly developed protective instincts where women are concerned—a legacy of being suddenly made the man of the family so young, I suppose—but he also has a deep respect for female strength, which I flatter myself is because of me. I may be small and delicate-looking but I'm tough—I had cervical cancer when Melissa was a baby, but it was caught early and I'm a fighter; I faced up to it and beat it. I think when Ryan met Ava he saw a woman like me—someone delicate, gentle, and with a core of steel that he could rely on in adversity. But the way that Ava acted at the wedding, and afterwards, well... I suspect that Ryan might have mistaken quietness for depth, and that she wouldn't have had the resilience to cope with Ryan when he was in a towering temper, which is not infrequently, or to stand up to him when his arrogance needed taking down a peg or two. Would that be an accurate assessment of her, do you think?'

Treasuring this glimpse into the complexity and contradictions of the man she loved and yet found so difficult to understand, Jane met the perceptive hazel gaze in the mirror.

'If you're asking did I think they were unsuited,' she said carefully, 'then, yes, I thought they were *deeply* unsuited.' And her tone suggested that was as much as she was prepared to say.

Peggy nodded. 'Tell me, just out of interest, what would *you* have done, Jane, in those circumstances? If some other woman had tried to stop *you* from marrying Ryan at the brink of the altar…?'

Jane swung around, blood in her eye, and Peggy rose with a quietly satisfied smile.

'Quite. Pistols at dawn rather than lady-like hysterics. Well, goodnight, my dear. Sleep well. And I suggest you lock your door if you consider you've already said a sufficiently polite goodnight to my son!'

Jane blushed…but did as Peggy suggested. She was deeply grateful for this unexpected gift of Peggy's moral support—whatever her motives might be—for without it she knew she could easily become a victim of her own desires. Drained by the upheavals of the day, she fell into bed and slept like a log, blissfully unaware of Ryan's soft tapping on the door an hour later.

The next morning followed the pattern set the previous afternoon, with Ryan's suggestion of a drive over to Karekare and a walk amongst the towering black sand-dunes overridden because Peggy wanted to look at the fashion sketches that Jane had mentioned at dinner.

She was encouragingly enthusiastic, and when she learned that Jane had been a keen sewer at school and was eager to take it up again she offered to give her a refresher course when her hands had healed enough to handle scissors and pins. Whisked up to the sewing room off Peggy's bedroom, Jane admired the state-of-the-art electronic overlocker and sewing machine, and shyly confided her dream of one day making a living out of sewing her own designs for sale at the markets, or in one of Auckland's many individualist boutiques.

Melissa mooched in on them and found herself reluctantly drawn into a discussion about the designers she liked. Shut out by a conspiracy of female opinion, Ryan gave up and retreated to the downstairs library that he used as an office.

At lunch he was surly and made no enquiry as to what Jane intended to do afterwards, an attitude that was explained by the arrival of Carl Trevor carrying a bulging briefcase. The women went down to the beach, and when they came back to find Carl's meeting with Ryan dragging on into the evening Peggy invited him to stay the night in comfortable tones of long familiarity. He accepted with an alacrity that was regarded sourly by his chief, especially when he produced an overnight bag from the boot of his BMW.

Recalling their two previous encounters, Jane was highly embarrassed to be seated next to Carl at dinner, but he smoothly exerted himself to put her at ease and she was soon laughing at his sardonic wit, relaxed enough to tease him about his jaded view of the world and joke about her newly acquired homesteading skills.

Peggy's maternal authority held sway, and Ryan and Melissa were briskly dispatched to do the dishes while Carl stretched and complained about the kinks in his back from an overly enthusiastic session at the gym that morning.

'Why don't you hop in the spa pool?' said Peggy, indicating the tiled round pool sunk into the lower level of the terrace on which they sat. 'A hot soak is probably what you need to loosen you up.'

'Good idea—Jane?'

She was frankly envious. 'Oh, I couldn't—my hands... Besides, I haven't got a bathing suit,' she said wistfully.

'I have plenty of spares for guests...there's bound to

be one your size. And you can fold your arms on the edge to keep your hands out of the water. Carl will be there to catch you if you slip. Go on, Jane,' urged Peggy. 'It's a wonderfully relaxing way to watch the sun go down.'

And so it was—until Ryan reappeared to find his personal adviser advising a giggling Jane on how to keep her straw in her glass of wine as she was buffeted by the bubbling water jets.

'Come to join us, Ryan?' grinned Carl, floating on his back in the water, his lithe physique outlined by the underwater lights.

Ryan's eyes glinted over Jane's body, encased in what she *had* thought was a very modestly cut black swimsuit. Her hair was twisted into a knot on the top of her head but steamy tendrils were escaping to corkscrew around her glistening face. She was flushed from the heat, her dark lashes spiky with moisture and her perpetually serious expression softened by the damp feathering of her thick eyebrows and the laughter lingering around her mouth.

Standing at the edge of the pool, the tip of his shoes almost touching the towel on which her hands rested, Ryan seemed impossibly tall, and as Jane tilted her head back to look up into his face she inadvertently gave him a swooping view straight down into the scooped neck of her swimsuit, where her creamy breasts, buoyed by the water, jostled for room against the tautly straining fabric.

'I want to talk to you.'

He had the gift of making a simple statement sound ominously like a threat, but Jane felt safe with Carl at her back. He, at least, didn't tangle her up in emotional knots and make her think sinful thoughts.

'So...talk,' she said with an airy shrug of her pale, gleaming shoulders that made her breasts bob gently on the surface of the water as Carl swam up beside her to take a sip from his glass of wine.

A muscle jumped in Ryan's jaw. 'Not here. Inside. Now.'

'But I'm not ready to come out,' she pouted, encouraged by his clipped restraint. He obviously wasn't going to risk a scene in front of his PA. 'Carl and I are working out our kinks, aren't we, Carl? Your mother recommended it. You should try it, Ryan, you strike me as a man with an awful lot of kinks—'

'Uh-oh...'

She barely had a chance to register Carl's breathy sing-song of amused warning as Ryan bent down, grasped her under the armpits and hauled her startled body out of the water with barely a grunt of effort.

'Is this kinky enough for you?'

Suspended from his grip, Jane flapped like a landed fish. 'Ryan!'

Ignoring the water sheeting off her body and Carl's laughingly ineffective remonstrances, Ryan carried her in through the open French doors and across the wide hall.

'Ryan, I'm dripping all over the carpet!' she protested in vain as they reached the library and she was set down with a jolt.

'Don't think you're going to use Carl to make me jealous!' Ryan growled, his hands remaining where they were, firmly compressing the sides of her breasts, his dark blue trousers and shirt showing the wet imprint of her body.

His anger was like the flick of a velvet whip. 'For goodness' sake!'

'I hired him, I can fire him,' he snarled. 'Bear it in mind that the next time you feel like flirting with him you could be costing him his career!'

'You wouldn't fire an employee for flirting with me, especially not Carl!' Jane scoffed, with an absolute conviction that sparked a small flame of appreciation in his angry eyes.

He dropped his hands but remained standing between Jane and the door. 'No, I wouldn't—because I'm not the cruel bastard you like to pretend to yourself that I am. And I didn't say he was flirting with you; I said *you* were flirting with *him*.'

'I was just being friendly—'

'Semi-nude over a couple of glasses of wine? A man could get the wrong idea about a woman that way.'

She wanted to dispute the semi-nudity, but suddenly realised that it would be a mistake to attract his attention to her treacherous body.

'Are you accusing me of being drunk?' she demanded belligerently. He knew full well that she had been in no danger of Carl misinterpreting her friendliness, but he was still furious. There was only one explanation for his unreasonable attitude: he was jealous!

Jane's burst of triumph was swiftly followed by a deep resentment. He had even less right than reason to feel jealous!

Ryan had planted his hands on his hips, his legs astride. 'No, just stupid—if you think I'm going to let you get away with it! This is between you and me, Jane. I won't let you hide behind another man, no matter how innocent the situation. If you want to flirt, why don't you flirt with the man you *really* want to hop in the sack with?'

Her resentment was goaded into temper. 'Why, you arrogant—'

'That's right, sweetheart, get mad,' he interrupted, running his gaze insolently down her body, allowing it to linger on her hard nipples, clearly visible against the thin nylon. 'I like it when you get hot and bothered over me.' She trembled and a wicked smile softened his angry expression. 'Hard to fight the memories, isn't it, Jane?'

Something inside her snapped. 'You should know!' she flung at him. 'You're the one who can't let go of the past!'

His dark head went up, as if catching a scent on the wind. 'What do you mean by that?'

'Ava!'

The name shimmered accusingly on the air between them.

'What about Ava?' he said, with a careful casualness that didn't fool her for a moment.

'Well, she's still your ideal woman, isn't she?' sneered Jane, wrapping her arms around her rapidly cooling body, her voice dripping with sarcasm as she whipped herself up into a jealous rage. It was as if Ryan's irrational burst of jealousy had given permission for hers to exist, and finally she was free to allow the old, corrosive envy that she had tried so hard to hide from her best friend to bubble to the surface.

'She's the oh-so-fragile flower of feminine perfection that all others are measured by, the woman you loved and lost, your soul mate, the one whom you knew instantly on meeting was the woman for you—only, hey, guess what? It turns out that she isn't!' she said with sweet vitriol. 'She ends up marrying someone else so I guess you must have been mistaken. But you can't accept that. You can't let the memory rest in peace—you're still so hung up about her you're always asking me questions about what she did and why—'

'Hardly *always*. That must be your guilty conscience working overtime, Jane,' he ground out. 'It's not *her* actions—the what and why of what *she* did that I'm hung up on—it's making sense out of *your* involvement.'

But Jane was beyond making sense. Having set her jealousy free, she could no longer control the words spilling off her bitter tongue. 'Did talking to her again bring all your old feelings flooding back? Are you wondering whether you might get a second chance at your first love? If you're hoping that she isn't happy, forget it! She and Conrad have a good marriage.'

He uttered a black curse. 'I'm not the type to waste my life pining for a lost cause, and that's what Ava became the moment she got married—only three months after she left me!'

'Oh? Then why were you so disappointed that I hadn't told her we'd slept together? Did you hope I might tell her what a fantastic lover you were so that she'd finally realise what she'd been missing? Maybe, in the twisted logic of your revenge having sex with me is the next best thing to bedding my unattainable best friend,' she spat unforgivably, and when he lunged towards her in raw outrage ducked under his arm and ran—out into the hall and up the stairs, fleet of foot, unencumbered by clothing, splattering drops of water against the walls as she dashed around the landings, conscious of his pounding pursuit gaining on her at every stride.

She'd had enough of a head start to get to her room just in front of him, tears blurring her eyes as her fingers fumbled to shoot the lock a split second before the full force of his pursuing weight hit the door. She leaned back against it, gasping for breath, feeling the vibration of his pounding fists down the length of her spine.

'Go away!' she shouted desperately.

'Jane—open this door!' He punctuated his angry demand with a hefty kick.

Why? So he could punish her with his contempt for her ridiculous accusations? Or poke and probe with that horribly relentless, incisive mind into the painful reasons for her ignominious loss of control? She'd thought love was supposed to be an enriching, spiritually uplifting experience, not this cheap fairground ride of thrilling euphoria followed by sickening plunges into terrifying despair.

'No—go away!' she gulped, dragging an arm across her eyes. Surely he wouldn't dare break it down? But at least, if he did, she knew the noise would bring Peggy swiftly to the rescue.

His voice lowered and she felt a little bump against the back of her skull that suggested he was resting his forehead against the polished wood. 'Jane? What's the matter? Are you crying, sweetheart?' She could hear him reining in his angry impatience. 'Look, let me in. I don't want to hurt you—I just want to talk...'

She gulped back her tears. Sweetheart! How could he call her that? Her heart was as shrivelled as an old boot and it was his fault!

'Well, I don't! Go *away*! Or—or I'll scream over my balcony for your mother!'

Silence on the other side of the door. Jane smiled a watery, humourless smile. She pressed her ear to the wood and still had it there when she heard a scraping sound coming from the open glass door to her balcony and rushed across just in time to see Ryan launch himself in a flying leap from the narrow rail of the next balcony, at least two metres away. In the darkness he seemed to hover like a sinister avenging angel before swooping earthwards.

Jane screamed as his landing foot hit her rail and slipped off again, but the forward momentum of his upper body carried him over the barrier to crash on his haunches in front of her.

'Are you *crazy*? You could have been killed!' she shrieked angrily as he bounced to his feet, her hands moving helplessly over his arms and heaving chest as if to reassure herself that he was real.

'Nah...a broken leg or two at the most,' he said, with infuriating macho insouciance, capturing her wrists and pulling them around his thick waist.

Her heart was still pounding like a freight train. So was his, she realised as her breasts were crushed against the hard wall of his chest. 'You could have been killed,' she repeated shrilly, almost paralysed by the thought of losing him.

'Would you have cared if I'd crashed to my doom?'

he murmured, his hands sliding up her long, trembling back. 'Maybe you might have thought I deserved it...'

She shuddered, burying her head in the damp front of his shirt, her voice muffled with horror. 'What a terrible thing to say.'

'I know...we've both said some pretty horrible things to each other in this love/hate relationship of ours, haven't we? That's why I think you're right—we shouldn't talk, talk only gets us into trouble—and, besides, actions speak louder than words...'

And, so saying, he eased back so that he could slant his hands over her shoulders and hook his fingers into the straps of her wet swimsuit, tugging them gently down her arms to bare her breasts to the soft night air, the whiteness of her body accentuated by the contrasting band of black fabric.

The only protest she could summon was a sigh of longing as he bent to moisten the tight twin peaks.

'Shh...' He smothered her choked murmur with his mouth and picked her up, carrying her across to the soft bed and collapsing down on it backwards so that she sprawled on top of him. He reached out and turned on the bedside lamp without breaking off the kiss, and as the familiar, addictive taste of him began to saturate her senses Jane gave herself up to a primitive world of all-consuming passion, devoted to the physical expression of the love that she was too afraid to put into words.

She helped clumsily as Ryan wrestled his shirt and her swimsuit off, throwing them to the floor and tugging her thighs astride him so that he could cup her naked bottom and move her against his undulating hips in a way that made her squirm with pleasure and plead for more. He was about to give it to her when a sharp rap at the door froze them in the midst of their glorious, erotic abandon.

'Jane—are you all right in there? I thought I heard a scream?'

Jane reared up on her elbows, looking down in shocked embarrassment at the face of the man beneath her. Ryan's hard features were blurred by reckless passion, his mouth bitten red by her feverish kisses, his eyes glittering chips of blue diamond fire.

'Yes.' She tried again, her panicky voice louder as she responded to Peggy's anxious call. 'Yes...but it was nothing—I'm fine...'

There was a pause, and then a quiet, 'Are you quite sure?'

She could feel the tension that gathered in every straining muscle of the powerful body that supported her as Ryan waited for her answer. For her choice.

'Yes—yes, I'm sure,' she said starkly. 'You don't have to worry, Peggy...thanks.'

She felt a wave of joy sweep over her at the fierce exultation that ripped through Ryan's expression. As they heard his mother's soft footfalls retreat down the stairs his hand slid around the nape of her neck and slowly applied pressure.

'She knows you're in here with me,' she whispered, when her mouth was an inch away from his.

He grinned wickedly. 'Good, then she'll know not to disturb us until morning!' He nipped her lower lip, and their mouths eagerly clashed again as he tipped her body sideways onto the bed while he pulled off the rest of his clothes. When he was gloriously nude he lifted her back on top of him, uttering a guttural groan as the soft thicket between her legs caressed his belly and a moist, creamy warmth settled over his aching groin.

Long minutes of heated bliss followed, until Ryan finally caught her desperately seeking hands and rasped, 'No—let me do it...you'll hurt yourself this way...'

He turned her gently over onto her back, extending her arms out to her sides so that her wrists draped over the edge of the bed and bracing the soles of her feet flat against the bed on either side of his knees. Then he positioned her hips and, with his eyes fixed on her flushed and excited face, entered her in slow, steady increments until he was buried to the hilt. They both groaned as he withdrew and began the process all over again...establishing a slow, sensuous rhythm of measured thrusts that progressively accelerated until they were both wrenched to a breathless peak of explosive ecstasy, their voices mingling in hoarse cries of frenzied rapture.

Afterwards, as they lay in a satiated tangle of sweaty limbs, Ryan kissed her wounded hands reverently, each in turn. 'If we're this good now, imagine how much more intense the pleasure will be when you can use these again!'

'I guess this means we're having an affair after all...' Jane's smile was tinged with *tristesse*.

Ryan traced it with a provocative finger. 'Not necessarily...'

Jane's abused heart clenched in her chest.

'Not if we regularised the situation.'

The blood drained out of her face, rushing to restart her stalled heart. Shock made her whisper barely audible. 'What?'

'Well, if you married me, we could sleep together as often as we like without offending your puritan soul!' But he was laughing as he said it. He was joking—he had to be!

She recoiled. 'You never said anything about marriage!' Or love. Didn't a declaration of love traditionally come first?

He shifted back from her, an infinitesimal distance, still smiling, but with a wariness in the back of his eyes that deepened her sense of foreboding. 'Does that mean your answer would be no?'

She noticed the conditional tense. He hadn't actually asked her a question yet, had he? It had been more of an evasively phrased statement. All Jane's old insecurities came rushing back as she remembered the numerous false hopes that Ryan had taken delight in tormenting her with over the past two years. A love/hate relationship he had called it—but it was Jane who had done the loving and Ryan the hating. What if this was just another trap?

'I suppose, if I said yes, I'd find myself jilted at the altar. That would be the ultimate revenge for you, wouldn't it? To turn the tables and humiliate me in exactly the same way that I humiliated you—'

As soon as the words were out of her mouth she knew she had made a fatal mistake. Ryan's face turned to stone and he slid out of the bed as if it were contaminated.

'If that's honestly the way you feel then any relationship between us is obviously futile. You're never going to completely trust me, are you? No matter how many times I prove myself.' He swept up his clothes and began pulling them on, the tenderness of a few moments ago wiped away as if it had never existed.

'Oh, yes, you'll sleep with me...even have a blazing affair with me against your better judgement. But you'll always withhold yourself from true intimacy because you don't trust me to behave honourably. I'm not the one who's hung up on Ava—it's you! You want to be a martyr to the past? Fine! You keep your trust...and I'll keep my honour! I thought I'd found a woman of pride and courage, but it seems I was mistaken—you're just another lost cause!'

CHAPTER TEN

THE long black evening gown shimmered and swirled around her ankles as Jane sailed through the crowded hotel restaurant, ignoring the curious looks of startled recognition that followed her determined progress.

She could see Ryan in a tight knot of people near the centre of the room. Less than twenty-four hours ago he had been shaking with pleasure in the privacy of Jane's arms, teasing her about getting married. Now he was the quintessential public Ryan Blair, rubbing shoulders with the rich and famous, drinking champagne and making deals.

A lost cause, was she?

She'd show him courage!

It wasn't going to be easy; she knew that. He was going to be savagely uncooperative. He was angry and he was hurting and he had had the whole day to brood. She had offered a gross insult to his honour, his pride and his manhood.

She should have known that Ryan wouldn't flaunt the idea of marriage lightly. Given his traumatic experience with Ava, it was understandable that he might prefer to approach it obliquely, protecting himself with humour, his defences ready to snap into place at the slightest hint of rejection. He had never said he loved her, it was true, but that didn't necessarily mean that he *didn't*... She had never told him how *she* felt, either, and men were notoriously less articulate about their feelings than women.

Peggy had not been the only one to be shocked when she had woken up this morning to find that Ryan had driven back to Auckland some time during the night. He had left a brief note of farewell for his mother and sister and a sealed envelope for Carl. No message for Jane—which she supposed was a message in itself.

'What happened?' Peggy had asked her bluntly.

Jane, red-eyed with weeping, still hadn't been able to believe it herself. 'He asked me to marry him.'

'And you turned him down,' Peggy had sighed.

'Yes.' Her face had looked so tragic Peggy had nearly smiled.

'Why?'

Jane had blinked. She'd tried to think of some of the reasons which had seemed so utterly compelling the night before.

'I don't know,' she'd realised slowly, horror dawning at her own blind stupidity. 'He took me by surprise...I suppose there was a part of me that just couldn't believe that I deserved that much happiness...'

The part of her that was still too much her father's daughter—the little girl who had learned to expect emotional blows instead of affectionate encouragement, the 'plain Jane' who had been told she wasn't worthy of a mother's love...

Someone murmured something into Ryan's ear and he looked up. An intense flare of white-hot emotion flickered across his face when he saw Jane, and then he was watching her approach through veiled eyes, his expression terrifyingly impassive.

'Hello, Ryan,' she said huskily, coming to a halt in front of him, glad he couldn't see her trembling knees under the long black dress that she hoped he recognised—her battle dress!

She loved him. She could do this! She pinned on a dazzling smile as she confronted her lover, brutally attractive in his formal white jacket and black tie. Sexual electricity crackled between them as they measured glances.

He inclined his dark head in the parody of politeness

that he did so well. 'Miss Sherwood. Gatecrashing again?'

'Actually, no, this time I managed to get one of these.' She brandished the ticket that Carl had scrounged at Peggy's behest.

It had been Carl who had given Jane a ride back to Auckland that morning, after mentioning that Ryan's memo had included a reminder that he would be requiring his adviser at an important fund-raising dinner that he was scheduled to attend that evening. As soon as Jane had learned that the fund-raiser's venue was the same restaurant which had hosted the Spectrum Developments bash, she'd known exactly what fate decreed she must do. She only hoped the grand gesture wouldn't backfire on her this time!

So she had shamelessly borrowed money from Peggy that she might never be able to repay and got Carl to drop her off at the hotel where the fund-raiser was being held. She had booked a room and called Dr Frey, wickedly invoking Ryan's influence to get herself an urgent appointment during which he had reduced the taping on her broken hand and delighted her with the news that her burn no longer needed a permanent dressing. Then she had spent two hours in the beauty parlour, getting the full works, and an hour at the hairdresser. She had even bought a new pair of high heels, but the lucky black dress was her charm.

She was once again dressed to kill—or be killed...

'Did you cash in my cheque? Or perhaps you've acquired yourself another rich protector?' Ryan's cutting drawl drew the attention of all those in the vicinity who hadn't yet recognised that here was a potentially explosive encounter.

'Maybe I still have friends in high places,' she countered lightly, not wanting to get Carl into any trouble.

'As long as you're not counting on me being one of

them,' he said, lifting his champagne glass towards his mouth.

She didn't flinch at his studied indifference. 'No,' she said huskily. 'I'm counting on you being my husband.'

A fine tremor shook his hand and a small amount of champagne splashed out of his glass onto his white silk lapel. He brushed at it without taking his eyes off Jane's exotically made-up face.

'I beg your pardon?' His tone was neutral, giving her no hint of what was going on inside his head.

'I'm here to ask you to marry me,' she said steadily.

Ryan's dark eyebrows lifted.

'I'm sorry, could you repeat that? I don't think I quite heard what you said,' he drawled, looking pointedly at the semi-circle of fascinated faces which surrounded them.

Oh, God! Jane's chin tilted higher and her voice rose firm and clear above the surrounding hum. 'I said, Will you marry me, Ryan?'

Conversation stilled, more heads turned, and Ryan took a leisurely swallow of his champagne and considered his options.

'Why—are you pregnant?' he demanded, and a sizzle of scandalised excitement swept through their immediate audience.

Mortified colour swept into Jane's cheeks. In none of the possible scenarios she had rehearsed in her head had he asked *that*! 'No, of course not,' she gritted.

His eyes swept slyly over her waistline and he leaned forward, his voice dipping to a murmur for her ears alone. 'You might be, since I didn't use anything last night...'

Her temper fizzled with the knowledge that he was toying with her. She was showing him that she trusted him not to complete his revenge and he was playing games. 'Well, I wouldn't know yet, would I?' she bit out fiercely.

He straightened, playing to their audience again. 'So, tell me then, Jane—why should I marry you?'

'Because I love you,' she declared, tossing it out like a challenge. She would offer him her gift, and if he wanted to throw it back into her face then it would be *his* loss. But she believed he wouldn't. She *believed* that he loved her; she had to!

'I beg your pardon?' He cupped his hand around his ear, his blue eyes glittering with mockery. 'What was that you said?'

'I said, I love you!' She threw out her hands in a gesture of helpless surrender and shouted it to the restaurant ceiling. 'I love you! I love you!' She looked at him furiously. 'Are you happy now?'

'No, but I'm getting there,' he taunted, taking another sip of champagne, patently enjoying himself.

Red misted her vision. She had had enough. She snatched the glass from his hand and threw it onto the floor, ignoring the thrilled gasps of horror that erupted around them

'A simple "yes" or "no" will suffice, Ryan, and then we can both get on with our lives!' she flared. 'Now, are you going to marry me or not?'

'Can I think about it?'

'*No!*'

He shrugged, looking bored. 'Well, I suppose I'd better say yes, then, since I happen to love you to distraction.'

It took a moment to distinguish his words from his tone and expression. Her knees buckled. Ryan began to laugh.

Love and fury fountained up inside her. 'You—!'

She took a furious swing at him and he sidestepped, scooping her off her feet and lifting her high in his arms, whirling her around for a passionate kiss. Then, still laughing, he carried her across the restaurant with an ease that suggested to the parting crowd that her voluptuous body was as light as thistledown. Cameras dazzled, and Jane linked her arms around Ryan's neck, resigned to her fresh notoriety.

'I have a room here at the hotel,' she whispered in his ear as they approached the glass door which led into the hotel foyer. Her eyes flirted with his startled expression. 'Plan B was to lure you up there and seduce you if you proved difficult,' she admitted with a sultry smile.

He grinned, his face lighting with incredible warmth, and for the first time Jane saw a resemblance to his mother. 'And I was, wasn't I? So Plan B it is!'

He nodded at the man who held open the door for them. 'Thanks, Carl, remind me to give you a bonus...'

Jane received a sly silver-grey wink as they swept past and realised, 'You *knew* I was going to turn up here tonight...!'

'How do you think Carl got hold of a ticket?' he said wryly. 'They're as rare as hen's teeth at this late stage.'

She had wondered why his adviser had been so co-operative and informative when his job was to be the soul of discretion! Her thick brows lowered. 'So this was all just a set-up, a *test*...?'

He shook his head as he carried her across the foyer, much to the entertainment of the staff, and into a waiting lift. He set her down and looped his arms around her waist as the doors closed and she pressed the button for her floor.

'Let's just say it was a window of opportunity I left hopefully ajar. I was angry when I left Piha, not thinking quite straight—but I knew it wasn't finished between us, no matter what I said. I'd been trying not to rush my wooing—' His mouth curved as he heard her choked disbelief. 'Yes, I know it mightn't have seemed that way. But I thought I was being very patient, considering how badly I wanted you.

'With Mum running interference for you I was getting hellishly frustrated, and last night was so good between us I simply blurted it out like an idiot. I forgot that because of your father you might look on marriage to a dominating male as something to be afraid of, and that I was presenting you with a totally new idea that you would need time to get used to...'

'No, it wasn't that...' She debated waiting until they had reached her room, but with the lift to themselves there was no reason to put it off. 'It was because it *wasn't* new that I reacted so horribly...because it was something I'd refused to let myself even dream about for so long...since Ava...

'I know you loved her—' Ryan tried to interrupt and she put her burn-scarred hand quickly over his mouth, revelling in her new freedom to touch. 'Please, let me finish—you have to know this. I'm breaking a trust, but I want you to know that *your* trust is more important to me...'

He took her hand from his mouth and kissed it, and she found the courage to continue. 'Ava came to me the day before your wedding in a terrible state, telling me that she and Conrad had fallen in love and that she couldn't marry you after all...but she was afraid of what you and her family might do if she tried to call it off at the last minute. She was practically hysterical. She begged me for help—'

'So you said yes,' he guessed gently, cupping her hot cheek, his thumb stroking her mouth. 'Loyal Jane... What a price you paid for that friendship. When you give your trust you give it totally, completely and for ever, don't you?' He sounded deeply satisfied.

'You don't seem very surprised,' she murmured, her terrible revelation having evoked none of the rage she had expected.

'In hindsight, I'm not... There was no *excitement* between Ava and I...not the kind of instant spark there was between *us*.' He narrowed his eyes as they swept over her body, and she instantly felt singing of her blood in her veins. 'I think I was in love with the *idea* of Ava rather than the actual woman herself... My feelings for her were one-dimensional, whereas with you...'

His voice dropped abruptly. 'With you I get the whole gamut of emotions. I was more offended by the sight of you laughing with Carl than I ever was by the thought of Ava sleeping with someone else.' He shook his head at her. 'The more I got to know you, the more I began to question my interpretation of events... I wondered whether my being jilted had anything to do with the fact that Ava married so quickly afterwards. Was she pregnant?'

'No, but she told me she was to persuade me to help her.'

'*What?*' This time his reaction was satisfactorily outraged. The lift doors opened and Jane found herself hustled along to her room, where Ryan kicked the door closed and demanded, 'She did *what*?'

'She was desperate.' Jane excused her friend with a generosity all the more complete for her own recent resort to desperate measures. 'She told me afterwards that she was terrified I might refuse to help, so she lied about being pregnant to make me more sympathetic...and of course it did...'

'So she used emotional blackmail to get you to take the blame for her actions—'

'No, don't you see? That's what's so *awful*!' If she had been able to Jane would have wrung her hands; as it was she just had to wave them in anguish. 'That wasn't her idea at all—that was *me*! *I* was the one who came up with the idea of making a horrible scene at the wedding that would make it easy for Ava to cry off. Because I was secretly *glad* when she came to me begging to call off the wedding. I *wanted* to stop it—not just for her, but for *me*, for selfish reasons, because I didn't want her to marry you...I wanted you to marry *me*.'

She spun away, unable to look at him in case she was

forced to witness the dawning disgust in his eyes. 'So you see, you were right all along when you accused me of being sick with envy. But it wasn't because I was jealous of Ava having someone to love her; it was because that someone was *you*.'

Her blue eyes were wild with shame and grief at the memory as she paced up and down. 'I was in love with you and Ava wasn't—and I hated it that you couldn't see that, that you still seemed to want *her*, and I hated it that you made me feel like an unfaithful friend and that I couldn't stop myself being attracted to you. I felt so guilty that it somehow seemed that I *ought* to take the blame for her not marrying you, because I had somehow *wished* it to happen, and that having you despise me would be fitting punishment which would also destroy the terrible temptation to try to make you love *me*. Oh, it all sounds totally ludicrous now, but back then it made an ugly kind of sense!'

'Not ludicrous at all…just very human,' said Ryan, catching her as she restlessly roamed by, tugging her over to sit with him on the bed. 'We rouse such strong feelings in each other that it's natural to be afraid of being overwhelmed by them, and, of all the passions, fear weakens judgement most.

'You weren't alone in feeling confused back then, sweetheart. Even standing there at the altar, in total shock, I felt a shiver of relief that someone was stopping me from taking the drastic step of marrying a woman whom I respected more than I desired. I tried to smother the feeling in rage and denial, but that moment of self-betrayal haunted me, especially since it was somehow tied up with the fact that you were the one who had perpetrated the terrible lies about me.

'But the strange thing was that I felt more betrayed by *your* lies than by Ava's defection. When you said that you and I were lovers, it was as though you had translated my deepest, most private thought into a deed.

And even when I met you again, after I came back from Australia, that was part of the pleasure of punishing you—making you pay for the sin of my desiring, until I discovered there was even more pleasure in loving you...'

'We're quite a pair,' said Jane huskily, wrapping her arms around him. 'A matched pair. You know, I even welcomed your revenge in a horribly twisted way because it meant that at least I knew I wasn't forgotten, I was alive in your thoughts...'

'Oh, you were in my thoughts, all right,' he said, kissing her rumpled brow. 'All the time... And the thought being father to the deed, I couldn't leave you alone—*can't* leave you alone...' he corrected himself, his hands wandering over the luscious curves of the black dress. 'So you'd better be prepared for a lifetime of this kind of attention...'

Jane laughed as he tipped her back on the bed and began to kiss her breathless. She couldn't imagine a more glorious fate!

CHRISTMAS MIRACLES

really can happen, and Christmas dreams can come true!

BETTY NEELS,
Carole Mortimer and Rebecca Winters

bring you the magic of Christmas in this wonderful holiday collection of romantic stories intertwined with Christmas dreams come true.

Join three of your favorite romance authors as they celebrate the festive season in their own special style!

Available in November at your favorite retail store.

HARLEQUIN®

HARLEQUIN WOMEN KNOW ROMANCE WHEN THEY SEE IT.

And they'll see it on **ROMANCE CLASSICS**, the new 24-hour TV channel devoted to romantic movies and original programs like the special **Romantically Speaking-Harlequin® Goes Prime Time**.

Romantically Speaking-Harlequin® Goes Prime Time introduces you to many of your favorite romance authors in a program developed exclusively for Harlequin® readers.

Watch for **Romantically Speaking-Harlequin® Goes Prime Time** beginning in the summer of 1997.

If you're not receiving ROMANCE CLASSICS, call your local cable operator or satellite provider and ask for it today!

Escape to the network of your dreams.

ROMANCE CLASSICS

Don't miss these Harlequin favorites
by some of our bestselling authors!
Act now and
receive a discount by ordering two or more titles!

HT#25720	A NIGHT TO REMEMBER	$3.50 U.S.	☐
	by Gina Wilkins	$3.99 CAN.	
HT#25722	CHANGE OF HEART	$3.50 U.S.	☐
	by Janice Kaiser	$3.99 CAN.	
HP#11797	A WOMAN OF PASSION	$3.50 U.S.	☐
	by Anne Mather	$3.99 CAN.	
HP#11863	ONE-MAN WOMAN	$3.50 U.S.	☐
	by Carole Mortimer	$3.99 CAN.	
HR#03356	BACHELOR'S FAMILY	$2.99 U.S.	☐
	by Jessica Steele	$3.50 CAN.	
HR#03441	RUNAWAY HONEYMOON	$3.25 U.S.	☐
	by Ruth Jean Dale	$3.75 CAN.	
HS#70715	BAREFOOT IN THE GRASS	$3.99 U.S.	☐
	by Judith Arnold	$4.50 CAN.	
HS#70729	ANOTHER MAN'S CHILD	$3.99 U.S.	☐
	by Tara Taylor Quinn	$4.50 CAN.	
HI#22361	LUCKY DEVIL	$3.75 U.S.	☐
	by Patricia Rosemoor	$4.25 CAN.	
HI#22379	PASSION IN THE FIRST DEGREE	$3.75 U.S.	☐
	by Carla Cassidy	$4.25 CAN.	
HAR#16638	LIKE FATHER, LIKE SON	$3.75 U.S.	☐
	by Mollie Molay	$4.25 CAN.	
HAR#16663	ADAM'S KISS	$3.75 U.S.	☐
	by Mindy Neff	$4.25 CAN.	
HH#28937	GABRIEL'S LADY	$4.99 U.S.	☐
	by Ana Seymour	$5.99 CAN.	
HH#28941	GIFT OF THE HEART	$4.99 U.S.	☐
	by Miranda Jarrett	$5.99 CAN.	

(limited quantities available on certain titles)

TOTAL AMOUNT	$	_____
DEDUCT: 10% DISCOUNT FOR 2+ BOOKS	$	_____
POSTAGE & HANDLING	$	_____
($1.00 for one book, 50¢ for each additional)		
APPLICABLE TAXES*	$	_____
TOTAL PAYABLE	$	_____

(check or money order—please do not send cash)

To order, complete this form and send it, along with a check or money order for the total above, payable to Harlequin Books, to: **In the U.S.:** 3010 Walden Avenue, P.O. Box 9047, Buffalo, NY 14269-9047; **In Canada:** P.O. Box 613, Fort Erie, Ontario, L2A 5X3.

Name: _____
Address: _____ City: _____
State/Prov.: _____ Zip/Postal Code: _____

*New York residents remit applicable sales taxes.
Canadian residents remit applicable GST and provincial taxes.

Look us up on-line at: http://www.romance.net

HBKOD97